NEW HAVEN PUB

W9-CJN-476

NEW HAVEN FREE PUBLIC LIBRARY

3 5000 09502 4203

DATE DUE

FEB 6 1985	MAR 24 1992	
DEC 2 6 1984	JUL 1 0 2002	
MAR 5 1985	DEC 1 2 2005	
MAR 2 8 1985	JUN 1 9 2006	
MAR 2 8 1985	MAR 3 0 2010	
JUN 1 7 1985		
NOV 2 8 1985		
JAN 2 4 1987		
D.S. MITCHELL LIBRARY		
MAR 7 1988		
D.S. MITCHELL LIBRARY		
JUL 5 1989		
MAR 1 - 1990		
MAY 1 2 1990		
JUN 2 1990		
AUG 9 - 1991		

OFFICIALLY WITHDRAWN
NEW HAVEN FREE PUBLIC LIBRARY

FEB 2 8

The Sheriff
of Bombay

The Sheriff of Bombay

H. R. F. KEATING

PUBLISHED FOR THE CRIME CLUB BY
DOUBLEDAY & COMPANY, INC.
GARDEN CITY, NEW YORK
1984

All of the characters in this book
are fictitious, and any resemblance
to actual persons, living or dead,
is purely coincidental.

Library of Congress Cataloging in Publication Data
Keating, H. R. F. (Henry Reymond Fitzwalter), 1926–
The sheriff of Bombay.
I. Title.
PR6061.E26S5   1984   823′.914
ISBN: 0-385-19461-7
Library of Congress Catalog Card Number 83-27295

Copyright © 1984 by H. R. F. Keating
All Rights Reserved
Printed in the United States of America

First Edition

Author's Note

Many distinguished citizens of Bombay, film stars even, have held the office of Sheriff. Needless to say, the person at the centre, the dead centre you might call it, of this story is not any one of them but the purest figment only of my fevered imagination.

The Sheriff
of Bombay

1

From the very beginning Inspector Ghote had no doubt about the identity of the killer. His anxieties and embarrassment arose only from the thought of making the arrest and the outcry it was bound to bring.

And the worst of it, he thought when he looked back from the height of his troubles, was that he had been sitting at his desk before it had all started worrying that of the full number of major crimes recently committed among the seven million inhabitants of Greater Bombay not one had been allocated by the Assistant Commissioner, Crime Branch, to himself.

Did the A.C.P. believe he could not cope with a difficult investigation? Was that why he had been landed with this unending and unsatisfactory business of the chain-snatching case at City Light Cinema? Dammit, it was a matter for the men out at Matunga only. If the victim, lured to a dark corner by the promise of a black-market ticket when the "House Full" boards were up, had not been the son of a major general in the Army, the theft of his neck chain, even though it was platinum and worth rupees six thousand, would never have come to C.I.D. Headquarters at all.

And he himself would never have been faced with hours of troublesome investigation, just as prolonged, just as detailed, as if it were a first-class murder affair, and with little chance, as everyone knew, of final success. A gang of chain-snatchers, once they had got hold of a prize like that, would make off fast and lie low, perhaps in their native place hundreds of miles out of Bombay. But despite this, because the victim was the son of a man with a high position in society—why, the matter might go up to the Legislative Assembly even—every possible witness had to be hunted out and questioned.

Arre, it was almost more work even than a murder case.

He had actually been about to hoist himself up from his chair and go off again to Matunga and that little lane behind the City Light

Cinema to try once more to dig out a decent witness when his telephone had rung.

"Ghote."

"A.C.P. here. Come up, Ghote. I've got something for you. Something I'd take on myself only I'm tied to this bloody desk all day."

"Yes, A.C.P. Sahib. Straightaway, A.C.P. Sahib."

Something so important that the A.C.P. would like to be handling it himself? What could it be? A major inquiry. Definitely a major inquiry. Perhaps he had all along been being kept in reserve for a major inquiry.

He leapt to his feet, gave one swift glance to the small square of mirror that hung on the far wall of his cabin, brushed a somewhat sweaty hand over his hair, pulled his shirt a little straighter and left almost at a trot.

Only at once to encounter Inspector D'Sa.

Grizzled, long-serving Inspector D'Sa, one of the last of the breed of Anglo-Indian and Indian Catholic officers who long ago at the time of the British Raj as well as in the years afterwards had been the backbone of the Bombay force. Inspector D'Sa, on the verge of retirement, stuffed deep and spilling over with memories of days gone past and liking nothing better than to pour them out over anyone he could manoeuvre into listening. Inspector D'Sa, his own particular bugbear.

"Ah, it is you, young Ghote."

"Yes, yes, D'Sa Sahib. But I am very much in a hurry. A.C.P. Sahib—"

"You remember I was telling you only yesterday, man, about how things used to be in Bombay? About how high moral standards were, even among the natives. Begging your pardon, young Ghote."

"That is quite all right, D'Sa Sahib. I am very much allowing for the way you were taught in your community in the old days. But, please, I must—"

"I won't keep you a minute, man. My God, have you youngsters got no politeness nowadays?"

"But—But a very important task is—"

"I just want to show you one thing, Ghote. Something that proves my point right up to the hilt."

"Well, yes. Then what is it only?"

"Look, man. Look at this."

From the top pocket of his plain-colour bush shirt D'Sa took a small flat object. He held it out in the palm of his hand.

Ghote looked down. It was a picture, a tiny, crudely coloured picture of a woman, a Western woman it looked like, dressed in a short red skirt and a bright blue blouse.

"Well," he said, after a little, "I am not seeing anything altogether proving what you are saying about old-days morals, D'Sa Sahib. A picture of a girl only. And now I must—"

"No, look. Look, man, look."

D'Sa twisted his upraised palm to and fro.

"Now do you see?" he asked.

Ghote saw.

The picture was evidently one of those trick ones covered with clear plastic strips in such a way that you saw one thing looking from one angle, something different looking from another. In this case the slight shifting in D'Sa's palm had simply stripped the girl of all her clothes.

"Well, yes," Ghote said. "I suppose such a picture would not have been seen in Bombay when you first came into the service, Inspector."

"No, it would not. And where do you think I got hold of this, man?"

"I am having no idea whatsoever. But, D'Sa Sahib, the A.C.P. himself—"

"A boy was selling them, Inspector, selling such displays of flesh and obscenity on the footpath in Hornby Road, not one hundred yards from this Headquarters."

Ghote experienced a momentary impulse to point out to Inspector D'Sa that the name of the street had long ago been changed to Dadabhai Naoroji Road and that nowadays almost everybody called it D.N. Road, and to add as well that measures in yards had been officially replaced by metres many years ago. But he knew that to do so would only get him embroiled in yet other arguments.

"Well," he said instead, "that is not really so terrible, Inspector. In Hutatma Chowk they are selling on the footpath sex cassettes, from England also. And, so they tell, in them you are made to hear all the sounds of intercourse taking place."

"The vendors should be whipped, Inspector," D'Sa broke out. "Whipped in the open *maidan.*"

He gave a sharp, reminiscent laugh.

"At least my toe connected with the backside of that boy in Hornby

Road," he said. "And sent every one of his filthy pictures into the roadway except the specimen I kept to show you, man."

Ghote thought of the boy's little stock of merchandise brought to sudden ruin. But again he checked a comment.

"Yes, yes, but I must be going to the A.C.P.," he said, turning away.

"Quite right, Inspector. Never keep a superior officer waiting. That's the way I was brought up in the days when the police service was the police service."

But Ghote was already at the entrance to the winding stone stairway leading up to the veranda outside the A.C.P.'s office.

Just as he was about to step into its coolness he heard D'Sa call out again.

"Oh, Ghote. One thing more. The Police Vegetable and Flower Show, I would want some help—"

Ghote poked his head back into the sun.

"Sorry, Inspector," he called. "Too much of work-load now."

Let old D'Sa organise the Vegetable and Flower Show on his own. That was about all he was fit for these days.

He took the winding stone stairs at a run, hurried along to the A.C.P.'s door, paused one instant to draw breath, looked in through the glass panel in the door, saw that the A.C.P. was unoccupied, knocked once and went in.

"Ah, Ghote. Good man."

Ghote clicked his heels to attention in front of the A.C.P.'s wide semicircular desk.

What was the task he was about to be assigned? The task that the A.C.P. himself would have liked to have taken up?

"The swashbuckler, Inspector. That mean anything to you?"

The swashbuckler. The swashbuckler. Had he misheard? What could the A.C.P. be talking about? The only Swashbuckler he had ever known of, and that had been long ago in his teenage days, had been a British film star, called then by all his friends, who did not fail to see each and every one of his pictures, invariably the Svashbuckler. But Swashbuckler or Svashbuckler, the A.C.P. could not possibly be referring to that figure of old.

"A film star, Inspector. British film star. I should have thought you'd have at least heard of him. I'd have hoped you'd have had the guts to bunk the class in those days and go and see his films."

"Yes, sir. Film star, sir. The Svashbuckler, sir."

He had had the guts, once or twice, when he should have been in class to pass through the classic-arch entrance of the old Edward Cinema and sit, feet tucked comfortably under him, watching hypnotised the Svashbuckler's daring feats until the moment came when, with the tension suddenly released, he in common with almost all the young audience felt impelled to jump up on his seat and cheer. But he could hardly claim still to have those guts.

"The fellow's here, Ghote."

"Here, sir?"

He actually took a quick look round the A.C.P.'s big, airy office to see if this mythical figure was somewhere in the room, concealed perhaps behind the screen that hid the cot on which in times of emergency the A.C.P. slept? Or sitting quietly, unnoticed till now, in the shadow of the big standing fan underneath the huge wall map of Bombay and its police districts?

"Not here, Inspector. Not in this room. In the city. Here in the city. Camping at the Oberoi-Sheraton."

"Yes, sir. Of course, A.C.P. Sahib. At the Oberoi-Sheraton Hotel."

Of course a big star, a real hero, like that would be at the Oberoi. Or shouldn't he rather be at the Taj? Wasn't a hotel like the Taj Mahal, built in the British days, somehow more in keeping? But no doubt he had chosen the newer, more modern, more American place for some good reason.

"We've been asked by the Minister of State for Home to show him round Bombay, Inspector. Before he goes off for *shikar* somewhere."

"Oh yes, sir."

Going off to shoot game was much more the idea of the man he had in his mind. Once it would have been tiger. Hadn't he gone after a wounded tiger single-handed in one of his films? But those days were long gone. The tiger was a protected national asset now. Yet no wonder the A.C.P. wanted to take on this duty himself. Such a famous star. To show him all the best of Bombay. It was hardly a first-class murder inquiry, but it was an honour all the same.

"Chap wants to see the Cages, Inspector."

The Cages. The notorious brothels that were at once Bombay's boast and its shame. Of course, they were a tourist attraction. Guidewallas who got hold of innocent visitors always made a point of

taking them there. But all the same. For the Svashbuckler to be taken
to see them. For such a hero. Such a White Man. Such a god. It was
not at all the right thing.

"But, sir—But, A.C.P. Sahib—"

"Yes? Yes, what is it?"

"Well, sir, are the Cages only a proper place for such a gentleman to
be seeing?"

"Good God, Ghote, are you embarrassed to do it? What is there to
be embarrassed? I myself—Well, as I was telling, I am one hundred
percent desk-bound. But the fellow wants to see the Cages, and see
them he will."

"Very good, sir. I would do it to my level best."

"I should hope so. Simple enough duty. And if you don't know your
way round in Kamatipura the fellows in Vigilante Branch tell me
there's a Dr. Framrose with a dispensary in Falkland Road. He looks
after the girls there, and is always ready to be helpful. Get him to take
you to the best place."

The A.C.P. gave a quick frown and a twitch of his moustache.

"That is to say the most decent place, Ghote. The most decent
place."

"Yes, sir. Yes, A.C.P. Sahib."

Inspector Ghote beat a hasty retreat.

But the embarrassment he felt was as nothing to what he was to
feel, dizzily dismaying, before his visit to the Cages with the Svashbuckler, that star of old, was over.

2

Embarrassments and complications seemed to pile up from the very start of Inspector Ghote's tour of Bombay's most notorious area as guide to Douglas Kerr, known to countless former small boys the world over as the Swashbuckler—and to former small boys in India as the Svashbuckler. Yet all were to pale into ridiculous insignificance before what came as the climax to the evening.

First there was the fact that in the Oberoi-Sheraton lobby, under its great lines of hugely elaborate twelve-foot-tall chandeliers, Ghote entirely failed to recognise the famous film star, his teenage idol. The Britisher who stepped out of one of the smoothly whirring lifts and stood looking round for him among the lengthy rows of aligned black leather sofas had longish grey hair in place of the dazzlingly fair short-back-and-sides that had singled out the Svashbuckler in his days of glory. His sagging, heavily flushed cheeks and thickened neck were related only remotely to the clean-cut good looks that had been the model and envy of all those boys of—was it?—twenty years before. And the nose, though straight and Greek godlike as ever, was red. Even purple.

At last, however, Ghote had been driven to realise that the semiwreck standing there looking about him must be his once-upon-a-time hero and had successfully introduced himself and led his charge out to the police vehicle and its patiently waiting driver. But conversation as they made their way through the still thick late-evening traffic towards the Kamatipura area was mined with unexpected difficulties.

"Is it you are pleased to be back once more in India, Mr. Douglas Kerr?"

"Prefer to be called Carr, if you don't mind, old boy."

"But, please, your name is being spelt K-E-R-R, isn't it?"

"Pronounced Carr. Surprised you don't know that, if you're as much of a fan of my work as you said you were."

"Oh, yes, indeed, Mr. Douglas Ker—Mr. Carr. I was always a very, very great admirer of your many feats."

"Only two, old boy."

"Only two feats? But I am thinking—"

"Feet. Feet, old boy. Things you have on the end of your legs, don't you know."

In a moment, or a little longer, Ghote had got the joke. He laughed. "Oh, jolly good."

A silence fell. Their driver honked viciously on the car's horn and squeezed up beside a long red double-deck bus and trailer. As they drew level a blast of searing fumes from its diesel exhaust came through the open window beside the Svashbuckler.

He flung himself half over Ghote on the rear seat beside him.

"Christ, what was that?"

"It is some exhaust fumes only. But, you see, if we are putting up the glasses next to us it would become altogether too hot inside."

The Svashbuckler resumed his upright, though slumped, position.

"I knew India wouldn't be exactly cool," he muttered. "But they told me this was the best time of year."

"Well, so it is, Mr. Douglas—Mr. Douglas Carr. November is the finest month in Bombay. But surely you must be remembering that?"

"Remembering? Why should I, old boy?"

"From your films. There were three of them picturised in India I am recalling, *The Svashbuckler Meets the Evil Kali, The Svashbuckler's Jungle Adventure* and *The Svashbuckler Meets the Evil Kali Again.*"

"Made in England, old boy. You don't think we'd come all the way out here just to shoot a few location sequences, do you?"

"But the tiger? When you went after the wounded tiger, single-handed only?"

"Few pots of plants in the old Denham studios, so far as I remember. Plus a bit of stock of some snarling brute or other. Magic of the movies, old son."

"Yes. Yes, I am seeing."

Ghote leant forward and rasped into the driver's ear.

"For God's sake, get a move on. Do you think we are in a funeral procession only?"

But complications were not over for him even when they reached Falkland Road and abandoned the car to make their way on foot through the thickly drifting crowds of prospective customers eyeing the girls who lounged against doorposts or, garishly dressed and thickly made-up, were looking out of the thin blue-painted protecting bars of the full-length, street-level windows, origin of the much-vaunted name of Cages. As they pushed past the gawpers and the vendors of food, balloons, pictures of the gods and a score of other things, suddenly above the tumult of the calls of the rowdier would-be customers and the insults flung back from the balconies of the battered wooden, slogan-daubed, advertisement-pocked old houses, above the blare of *filmi* music from the narrow little restaurants, above the squeaking of the vendors' bleating balloons, there came a shriller screaming cutting its way above everything. It drew Ghote's attention, and the Svashbuckler's.

There, outside one of the houses, was a Western woman of some considerable age, her short stringy body nondescriptly clothed in a cotton blouse and bleached-looking flowered skirt. She was holding open in front of her a large reporter's notebook, and from the balcony above, accompanied by that extra loud shriek of abuse, one of the girls had flung at her a bucket of water. Of water, or worse.

Ghote looked round, hoping that a patrolling constable might be there to sort out the trouble. There was not one anywhere in sight. He decided it was his duty to go to the rescue, little guessing that this chance encounter and the advice he was about to give would lead before very many days had passed almost directly to sudden death.

"*Ek* moment, please," he said to the Svashbuckler. "I must just find out what that Western lady is doing in this locality. She appears to be altogether in a soup."

"But—But, I say, old man, is it—Well, isn't it asking for trouble? I mean, those girls up there look pretty rough customers."

"Nevertheless," Ghote said, "the lady is a visitor to India only, and a lady also."

He had hardly time to reflect that the Svashbuckler's attitude was scarcely that of the man he had watched, long ago, entering bars in tough New Orleans, in wicked Surinam, in frozen Alaska to mop up whole roomfuls of sailors insulting his heroines before he had pushed his way through the bystanders and reached the lady with the notebook and, he saw, a well-soaked skirt.

"Madam," he said, "I am a police officer and you are seeming to be in grave troubles. May I ask what it is you are doing here? This is a very, very notorious area."

"I should hope it is," the girl's victim replied in a strongly accented American voice. "That's what I'm here for."

"But, madam," Ghote said. "Madam, the only class of women in this locality are—They are gay girls only, madam."

"Gay girls? Gay girls? Boy, I've heard whores called by any number of substitute terms since I landed in this country: 'magdalenes' and 'members of the ignoble profession' and 'crossers of the moral barrier' and 'women of doubtful character.' But that I do believe is the worst yet."

From behind his shoulder Ghote heard the Svashbuckler break out into a great bray of laughter.

"Nevertheless, madam," he said, determinedly addressing the lady with the notebook, "it remains true that this is an area devoted to prostitution only. It is not at all proper that you should be here."

She gave a sprightly look round about.

"Seems to me there are plenty of people here just to rubberneck," she said. "Just because all of them are males, doesn't seem any good reason why I shouldn't come too. Specially as I'm here for strictly scientific reasons."

"For scientific reasons, madam?"

Again Ghote heard a bellow of laughter from the aging British film star.

"I am a sociologist, I'd have you know, officer. Dr. Dorothy Ringelnatz, North Adams State. And I'm in Bombay to make a study of behavioural attitudes among Third World prostitutes. Tonight I was carrying out a little preliminary field-work—only the subjects seemed to object."

She looked down at her bleached old skirt, patched with a large area of wetness. Ghote confirmed through his sense of smell that what had been flung at this extraordinary visitor was not water.

"Madam," he said, "I would most strongly advise for you to secure the company of some Indian sociologist if you are wanting to make further visits to this area. But now, please, let me find for you a taxi. In what posh hotel are you staying, please?"

"Well, I guess you're right, officer. I can't say I've made much effective contact here tonight."

Dr. Ringelnatz closed her notebook with a definitive snap.

Ghote, to his great relief, spotted the yellow roof of a taxi halted to set down a pair of prospecting customers not far along the street. He shouted and waved and managed to catch the driver's attention.

"Well," came the Svashbuckler's loud tones as at last the cab's door closed on the rescued American, "I'll be able to dine out on that lady when I get back home, never mind the night that lies ahead."

The night that lies ahead. Ghote's heart sank. Was his hero of old really intending to do more than just look at the Cages and their occupants? And, if he was, what should his own attitude be? Would he actually have to stay there and wait for the girls' notable client in case, a fairly unlikely event in fact, he was robbed? And what about the rather more likely event of his catching an infection? What could he do about that?

But perhaps this Dr. Framrose whom the A.C.P. had suggested as a knowledgeable and reliable informant would be able to persuade the Svashbuckler to behave with discretion.

He set off along the crowded street in search of the doctor's dispensary, ignoring the shouted invitations from the blue-painted barred windows and dark doorways and hoping that the Svashbuckler was proof at least against the cheap allurements of the more blatant of the girls thrusting forward half-naked bosoms or turning to flick up short skirts—like the one worn by the girl in Inspector D'Sa's trick picture— to display cheeky behinds.

Tea boys with their newspaper cones of snacks and glasses of milky liquid clutched in strong fingers dodged away in front of them. Squatting circles of card-playing pimps and hangers-on glanced up angrily when they chanced to brush against their backs. Slow rivers of male humanity, young and old, the bare-chested and the well dressed, millhands and briefcase-clutching babus, flowing in counter-currents along the narrow thoroughfare, jostled them and swerved to either side to let them pass.

Then at last, just beyond the big Olympia Café, he spotted a painted sign on a wall proclaiming *Dr. Falli Framrose, Sexologist, F.R.S.H. (U.K.), Sex Diseases, Sex Changes.* He pushed his way towards the place, a wooden house as narrow and dilapidated as any other in the street, and no cleaner. But inside light shone brightly, and it looked as if the doctor was at least there.

Could he be relied upon to issue a sufficiently stern warning about the dangers of frequenting the houses of his neighbours?

Ghote stepped up into the barely furnished front room of the narrow house, the ex-film star at his heels.

Dr. Falli Framrose was not a person whose outward appearance immediately impressed. To begin with, his face and narrow bald skull were blotched all over with the dark patches of leucodermia, the skin disease that inbred Parsis often suffer from. Then he was, as well, fearfully thin, the very opposite of the picture of well-fed healthiness that a hundred film idols had established as the peak of desirability. Finally the large horn-rim spectacles he wore had slipped almost halfway down his long droopy Parsi nose in a manner which hardly gave the impression of high efficiency.

Ghote introduced himself and his distinguished visitor.

"Ah, yes. Come to see the sights, eh?" Dr. Framrose said in a high-pitched erratic voice. "Come to see the coupling and the copulating going full swing. You know what it all means to me? I'll tell you. Buboes and itches, sores and syphilis. That's what it all amounts to in the end, see it from my point of view."

Ghote took a quick look at the Svashbuckler. Yes, an expression of apprehension had appeared on the face that once had smilingly confronted any danger the magic of the cinema screen could produce. Well and good.

"My Vigilante Branch colleagues are telling that you would be the best guide to a decent brothel, Dr. Sahib," he said. "If you are able to take the time I would be very, very grateful."

"Yes, yes. I'll lead you to my good friend Heera's. She's as typical a *gharwali,* a madam, as you'll ever see."

He gave a cackle of laughter.

"That's to say," he added, "as rapacious, unfeeling and self-seeking a woman as you could find. Come along, come along."

From a nail on one of the pale green, decidedly scabby walls he plucked an old black umbrella and hung it down his back from his ridgelike left shoulder. But at the door he darted back in again.

"Drugs cupboard, drugs cupboard," he said. "Must make sure that's locked. They'd break in here and take every blessed thing out of it, poisons and all, if they thought they could get that open. You know that every man jack on this street is a thief, don't you?"

Ghote did not feel the need to confirm or deny the statement to his British companion. He watched the doctor plunge into an inner room and saw him test vigorously the doors of a strong-looking steel cupboard attached to its far wall.

Well, at least he seemed to have a good sense of responsibility. And he had put a first-class scare into the Svashbuckler.

"Now, sir," Dr. Framrose said, scuttling back into the room and addressing the film star, "you are a foreigner in a strange land. So let me tell you what we in India do for our *filles de joie,* of which shortly you will be seeing some prime specimens."

He pushed his slipped spectacles back up his long nose with a thin sliding finger and turned to Ghote.

"You are acquainted with that excellent work *The Ten Princes,* Inspector?" he asked.

"It is a film only?" Ghote inquired. "I am not seeing many films nowadays, I regret."

His answer seemed to please Dr. Framrose, at least to judge by the vigour of his cackling laugh.

"Work of prose, Inspector," he said at last. "Work of prose from the seventh century, one of the glories of our Indian heritage. Now, sir . . ."

Out in the street, amid the raucous blare of two or three different *filmi* tunes emanating from the open-fronted restaurants on either side, with the sound of quarrels and the whistlings and croonings of feminine enticement, with the tea vendors' cries of *"Chai . . . Biscoot"* loud in their ears, the doctor seized the Svashbuckler by the elbow and, hurrying him along, retailed the ancient wisdom in a voice that swooped and soared as high and low as the massed violins and cascading silvery *jal-tarangs* of the music all around.

"The duties of the mother of a courtesan, sir. As told by the sage of old. One, to provide nourishment from the earliest age to develop stateliness, vigour, complexion and intelligence while at the same time harmonising the gastric calefactions and the secretions. Then, instruction from the fifth year in the arts of flirtation, major and minor. A conversational acquaintance with grammar—most important that— and profound skill in money-making, in sport, in betting on fighting cocks and games of chess. Next, obtaining wide advertisement for her charms and beauty through astrologers and others and finally raising her price to the highest when she has become an object of general desire."

They came to a halt in front of a house no more dilapidated than the others, its doorway no darker, the girls behind the bars of the ground-floor room as brazen.

"Now, sir," said the doctor loudly. "Take note, all this at street level is of no concern to our good *gharwali* Heera. She operates on the floor above. A much more select establishment. There you will be able to observe the gastric calefactions and the secretions at their most charming, and I myself shall take the place of the astrologer in praising their particular beauties and skills."

Ghote began rapidly to alter his opinion of Dr. Framrose. Was he not positively encouraging his distinguished visitor to debauchery now? To dangerous debauchery?

As they were about to enter the narrow doorway, where on a bench under the light of a paper-garlanded, fly-blown electric bulb, sat three girls from the establishment above, one of the whores from behind the bars reached out and caught at Ghote's arm.

"Ten rupees only," she cooed.

He shook her off and began to follow the doctor and the big shambling Britisher inside.

"Eight rupees," the whore called out after him more loudly. "Six. Four. Two. Four rupees on the cot, two only on the mat."

Ahead there was a narrow flight of ill-lit stairs, steep almost as a ladder. In the wake of the others he set foot on them. It was when he was nearly at the top that there occurred the incident that was almost completely to overwhelm him with the perplexities it brought in its train.

There was a passageway straight in front with three flimsy partition doors off it. Only the weak light coming through a window behind them illuminated it, and his view was partially blocked by the tall figure of Dr. Framrose and the bulkier one of the Svashbuckler. But, as his head had come level with the bare boards of the floor, his attention had been attracted by a sharp scuffling at the far end.

Stepping up higher, he had seen, or half-seen, in the gloom two people. One of them, the nearer one to him, was a woman, a huge fat creature dressed in a gaudy red sari with a wide gold border. And the other, beyond her and all but hidden by her, was a man.

There was something furtive about the pair of them, hurried and furtive, that kept his attention fixed, the unconscious reaction of a trained police officer. The fat woman was pushing the man energetically in front of her and he was in part, it seemed, yielding to her and in part playfully resisting.

It was only at the last second, before the two of them disappeared round the far corner, that, in a stray beam of light coming from a gap at the top of the furthest closed door, he saw for one instant, clearly as if caught in a torch ray, the man's face.

And it was a face he knew, knew well though he had seen it only in photographs. But that face had been photographed many, many times. It was the face of one of the city's most prominent people, the man who was currently the Sheriff of Bombay.

3

The Sheriff of Bombay. Ghote felt a hot prickling spread right up into
the roots of his hair. To have caught such a distinguished citizen in
such a place as the *gharwali* Heera's brothel. Why, it was not even as if
this was one of the most respectable houses in the area. Of course, it
was not any of the really cheap places, the ones in 8th, 9th, 10th,
11th, 12th and 13th Kamatipura Lanes. They were the very bottom.
But neither was it one of the houses in Sukhlaji Street, or Safed Galli,
Whites Lane, as it had been called when the European and half-caste
prostitutes had congregated there in the days of the British Raj. If
someone like the Sheriff was going to come for such purposes to this
area at all, and not to one of the few discreet posh brothels in respectable parts of the city like the place on top of Tardeo Air-conditioned
Market that the Vigilante boys had raided not so long ago, then it
should have been to Sukhlaji Street or perhaps to one of the num-
bered houses in Foras Road.

And yet he himself had distinctly seen him—Was it the Sheriff? Yes.
Yes, he could not mistake that well-known face—sneaking off towards
some doubtless vile-smelling back way out of the house. The *gharwali,*
who surely was the fat creature in the red sari, must have heard Dr.
Framrose's loud, high-pitched voice talking to the Svashbuckler as they
were about to enter and have hurriedly escorted away her distinguished client.

Her distinguished client. And he was distinguished indeed. Doubly
so. First, he was the Sheriff of Bombay.

Ghote had read once in one of the papers when a film star had been
given this high municipal office that it ranked third in order of social
precedence in the city. It was an annually held office dating from the
British days, like such posts as the Protonotary and Senior Master of
the Admiralty and Ecclesiastical Registrar, and its duties were largely
honorary. At the Quarterly Court of Sessions it was the Sheriff's task

to call on the various accused to rise and to read out the charges. It was also his official duty to execute the decrees of the High Court, although in practice these were attended to by his staff. But unofficial duties the Sheriff had by the hundred. He was expected to meet and greet visiting dignitaries to Bombay. He was begged to open important new buildings, to inaugurate large-scale commercial functions, to be the chief participant at the ceremony releasing the occasional important book, to preside over the city's most prestigious annual prizegivings.

If the present holder of the office had been no more than that, some huff and puff fellow who had given useful political service to the party in power and had been granted his reward, the situation would have been embarrassing enough.

But the present Sheriff was much more than this. He was almost as much a figure of renown as a top film star. He was the Rajah of Dhar, until not so long ago captain of the Indian cricket team. A hero to the Bombay crowds who, come each Test series, are fired with wild enthusiasm for the strange game the British introduced to India's shores, fired with enthusiasm from the richest businessmen abandoning their luxury offices and paying extortionate sums for a seat in the Wankhede Stadium down to the meanest barefoot coolie padding the streets under his head-load and striving to overhear the interminable commentary from one of the myriad of transistor radios clamped to the ears of those slightly better off than himself. Why, even his own son, even little Ved, had a photograph of Randhir Singh, Rajah of Dhar, pinned up by his bed, and referred to him familiarly as Randy.

And this was the man he had seen sneaking out of a low-class brothel.

Ghote stood where he was at the top of the flight of narrow stairs, looking transfixed along towards the darkness at the end of the passageway where the *gharwali* and the Sheriff of Bombay—it could be no other—had scufflingly disappeared. In front of him Dr. Framrose, the weak light from the open door glinting on his bald splotched skull, called out in his high, erratic voice.

"Heera. Heera, my dear. I have brought some valuable customers to admire the exquisite female flesh you have on sale. To admire only, I regret to say. They'll hardly bring you in a rupee. But then as one of them is a policewalla you'll doubtless be glad to be in his good books."

There came no answer from the far end of the passage. Dr. Framrose set out towards it.

"Heera, Heera. Whatever are you doing out there? You'll catch some dangerous illness, let me tell you. The back of your house is notoriously unhygienic."

So, Ghote thought, the doctor has not recognised the Sheriff. If he had, he would hardly be pursuing the fat old *gharwali* in the way he was doing. She would not thank him if he stopped her whisking away that high personage so unfortunately caught out.

But, of course, the Parsi was probably half-blind, and those spectacles of his must have slid right down to the end of his long nose.

And another thing. The Svashbuckler, who had after all never visited India before, would be highly unlikely to know the Sheriff by sight, even if once or twice he might have seen him playing when he had led the Indian cricket team to England.

He advanced further along the passage. The *gharwali* would return in a few minutes and the visit to her establishment must go on. Entertaining the Svashbuckler was his immediate duty, and he would carry it through.

Behind him on the stairs he heard footsteps. He turned and saw one of the prostitutes they had brushed past on the bench in the doorway. Was she coming up to make them an offer? If she did, she was going to get a pretty sharp firing.

But instead, it seemed, the girl had got herself a willing customer. A dark shadow was creeping up behind her, head turned sheepishly to the wall. The girl—she was, Ghote noticed now, a pretty enough thing, young, pleasantly plump and with an air of happy bright-eyed assurance about her—was evidently anxious to occupy the room behind the first of the ramshackle doors, all the while firmly shut.

"Kamla," she called out, loudly and clearly. "Hé, Kamla, what for are you still in there? Don't you know how to make a man do what he has to do? Come on. My customer can hardly wait, such a lion he is."

Ghote had some difficulty suppressing a laugh at this: the girl's customer, standing now three quarters of the way up the stairs and doing his best to shrink right into the dirty, betel-juice splashed wall beside him, looked anything but a lion.

"Kamla. Kamla. Come on."

There was still no response from behind the flimsy door. Nor had the fat *gharwali* reappeared from the far end of the passage.

"Kamla."

The little prostitute—she can hardly be more than sixteen or seventeen, despite the lively knowingness, Ghote thought—tired of waiting, grasped the top of the partition door with both hands and pulled her plumply rounded body up till her bare toes dangled.

Ghote heard her give a little gasp as her eyes came level with the wide gap at the top of the door.

She slid back with a thump on to the dirt-engrained boards of the passageway. Then she gave the three of them standing waiting for the *gharwali* a quick, sharp look.

Ghote could read the thought behind it as clearly as if he had been looking at a comic strip in one of the papers and the words had been written out in a balloon. It was a thought he had known applied to himself on countless occasions: *Policewalla, watch out.*

What had the girl seen, he asked himself, that a policewalla had better not know about? It could hardly be the customary scene that would go on behind that apology for a door. Police officers knew all about that, even participated in it often enough by way of receiving a gift from brothel madams and proprietors. And besides in the tolerated area it was not even illegal.

So what had the girl seen in that quick glimpse inside the room that had caused her first to gasp and then to go suspiciously silent?

Whatever it was, she was certainly not going to let out the secret. She was turning now to her poor, shame-faced client and telling him, with cheerful impudence, that he should be ashamed of himself coming to a house like this and that he had better get home to his wife before that lady lifted her *belna* from rolling out chapattis and hit him over the head with it. Next she turned and, pushing past Ghote and the others, head stuck in the air, disappeared round the corner at the end of the passageway where the *gharwali* and the Sheriff had gone.

Something is definitely wrong in that room, Ghote thought. But something serious? Or something best to ignore? He could not decide. He toyed with the thought of strolling back to the door and casually peering over its top in his turn. But, he realised, he would not be able to do so without standing on tiptoe, and the notion that he would be thought of as doing that in order just to observe the usual goings-on inside was not something he felt prepared to lay himself open to. The Svashbuckler had already shown too much willingness to laugh at him.

He was saved from making up his mind by the abrupt reappearance of the wobblingly huge *gharwali*.

"Doctor Sahib," she said, gently patting her fat hands together in a show of enormous pleasure. "Doctor Sahib, it is good to be seeing you. And these gentlemen, very, very good also."

She came simpering and waddling up to the Svashbuckler and favoured him with an immense smile, showing betel-red teeth filed to sharpness in wide gums.

"From Vilayat?" she said. "From England, isn't it? Ah, I am so glad to see English gentleman. Many, many have I had between my legs when I was a young, young girl only."

The Svashbuckler, who had been smiling back at her nearly as heartily, retreated a pace.

Well, Ghote thought, the idea of anyone being between the massively fat legs straining that red sari to splitting point was certainly not attractive.

"But you must have some tea," Heera breezed on. "Some tea, some cold drink, some *paan* to chew."

She advanced again on the Svashbuckler and looked at him roguishly.

"Perhaps the *angrezi* gentleman would like a bed-smasher *paan*," she said. "Something in it to lend force-force to him before the night is finish. Let us all go along to Olympia Café and have something. Perhaps stop at the *paanwalla* on the way, isn't it?"

"No, no, Heera, my dear," Dr. Framrose broke in. "We haven't come here just to be taken to that wretched eating place. We've come to see the full delights of your establishment, to fill these gentlemen's heads with thoroughly disturbing visions. And then take them off to safety before they can do anything to make fools of themselves. You know the way we always do it with the V.I.P.s the police send along. What on earth makes you want to take us to the Olympia?"

Yes, Ghote echoed in his mind. What does make you want to get rid of us? It cannot be the presence in your house of the Sheriff of Bombay. You have spirited him away neatly enough. What is it then?

Well, one thing was certain. Whatever it was, it was something to do with what that plump little prostitute had seen when she had peered over the door. She had been quick enough to go and fetch her madam when she had seen that, and Heera was determined enough to get all three of them out as soon as she possibly could.

He turned, took a few sharp steps back along the passage, put both hands against the mysterious door and gave it a good hard push.

It flew open, and at once he saw what had made the girl gasp.

It was a wonder she had not screamed.

On the bed that filled most of the narrow room there was sprawled the naked body of a woman, face down. And it was clear beyond doubt that she was dead, that she had been murdered. Round her neck, biting deeply in, was the mark of whatever it was that had been used savagely to strangle her. Her whole head was twisted to an angle that no living body could have sustained.

But there was more than that to make a fellow prostitute scream out. All down the back of the body were the deep weals of a brutal beating, the very cross-thongs of the coarsely plaited whip clearly visible.

Ghote, just inside the little room, was aware, as a small unnecessary irritation, that Dr. Framrose and the Svashbuckler had crowded into the doorway behind him. Then there was a sudden crashing sound and, as he turned, he saw that the Svashbuckler had swung round and was now vomiting comprehensively in the passageway outside.

That is all I am needing, he thought. A V.I.P. visitor put into my charge, and I have led him straight to the sight of an appalling murder. And now I shall have to get him back as soon as I can to his five-stars hotel and everyone in the lobby there will see him come in covered with his vomit only. And there is the murder also. It must be my duty to stay here to see that nothing is done to the body until an investigating officer from the Nagpada station can come. Because it is altogether certain that if Heera had succeeded to get us out then that little girl— what a cool head in one so young, what other terrible sights she must have witnessed in her short life—would have made damn sure the body disappeared before anyone else saw it.

He gave the *gharwali* a glare of rage for what she had attempted to do and then turned to Dr. Framrose as the most reliable person to hand.

"Doctor Sahib," he said, "you have seen that woman on the bed.

Undoubtedly she has expired. Do you have telephone in your dispensary? Can you call up the Nagpada police and inform?"

"Yes, yes, my dear Inspector. It will be a pleasure to assist our noble police in the performance of their duties, and perhaps also I could relieve you of this encum—Perhaps I could give myself the pleasure afterwards of putting Mr. Kerr into a taxi and even seeing that he gets safely back to his hotel. By the most discreet entrance, I think."

Ghote felt a waft of relief. At least that burden would be off his shoulders.

And then, as the doctor not without wild exaggerated gestures ushered the vomit-spattered Britisher down the narrow stairs and away, he realised that the Svashbuckler was by no means the most oppressive of his troubles.

What now weighed down on him was the possibility, perhaps even the certainty, that the brute who had inflicted those wounds on the girl in the room behind him, who had at last taken his whip and frenziedly strangled her, was none other than the Sheriff of Bombay. And, worse, he himself, and perhaps only fat Heera as well, was aware of the exact identity of the man who had been visiting the brothel when the frenzied killing had taken place.

Certainly Heera would never tell the investigating officer from the Nagpada station who it was who had been the murdered girl's last customer. The possibilities for magnificent blackmail would clearly be too tempting. Nor would she at all know that he himself had caught that one revealing glimpse of the well-known face. As to any of the girls in the house being in on the secret, it was unlikely. They would be among the few Bombayites who were hardly interested in cricket, even at the sensational Test match times.

No doubt, too, the Sheriff had taken pains on any previous visits to the house not to be seen by more of its occupants than necessary. He would have slipped in always, if he had indeed visited the place regularly, by the same insanitary back way through which he had been smuggled out. Perhaps even Heera knew no more than that the man who had patronised her house was someone rich and influential.

No, the presence of the Sheriff of Bombay in a brothel where a horrible murder had taken place, perhaps the fact that he had actually committed that murder, was something that he alone, by the merest of chances, had had entrusted to him by fate. And he knew at once without having at all to think it out that, despite the nature of the crime, there would be tremendous opposition to any attempt he might make to get the Sheriff brought in as a witness. As to trying to assemble a case against him, should no one else appear to have been the killer, the very thought was too overwhelming even to contemplate.

All because of that single, swift sight of a face. Could he forget that he had seen it? Was he sure enough that he had seen what he had seen?

What a mountain of tribulation to have resting on his own slight shoulders.

4

As Ghote stood in the doorway of the murder room staring unseeingly at the huge bulk of the *gharwali* blocking the narrow passage further along—and no doubt busily working out where her own best advantage would lie now that she had failed to get rid of her unwelcome visitors—a sudden thought came into his head.

Looking at that brutalised body he had seen, without in that first moment taking full note of it, something else.

He had seen the weapon.

He had seen the very whip which the killer must have used, first to flog his victim, then to strangle her. It had been flung carelessly back where perhaps it usually rested, a luxury item of the cheap brothel's equipment, across a pair of long nails crudely driven into the wall beside the door next to a garishly coloured calendar depicting the god Shiva and his consort Parvati, the pair of them almost as amorously bent as when Shiva had in legend ignored the greeting of the sage Bhrieu and had been transformed into a stone-pillar *lingam* for the insult.

And on the handle of the whip—there could be little doubt about it —would be what must link the killer to his deed. With scientific certainty.

Fingerprints.

True, they might be smudged. True, they might not be the only ones there. But the Fingerprint Bureau were extraordinarily skilled in deciphering smudges, in allocating overlays. If they had the prints of a suspect to check against, it was a very good bet that they would be able to produce proof. Proof that would stand up at a trial against even the wiles of the cleverest Defence advocate—perhaps one day in the Quarterly Court of Sessions when someone other than the present Sheriff of Bombay rose to read out the charge.

Yes, as soon as the investigating officer arrived from the Nagpada station, and that could not be long now, he would draw his attention to the whip. Perhaps it would be best even to make sure, with an officer possibly not as experienced as he might be in murder inquiries, that the fellow took the proper precautions over seeing that the transfer of such evidence to the Fingerprint Bureau was duly witnessed at every stage. If it was going to be the Rajah of Dhar who was to stand at last in the dock, every step in the prosecution case would have to be conducted altogether beyond the possibility of being undermined by the most cunning lawyers money could buy.

He saw that the little prostitute who had so level-headedly warned her madam had come creeping back from the rear of the house. Fat old Heera had seen her too.

"Munni," she said abruptly, "get water. The *angrezi* sahib was sick. Sweep it away."

So much by way of thanks for a warning cleverly given, Ghote thought, pitying the girl a little.

But she did not seem to feel she was being ill-rewarded. Without a word but without any sign of sulkiness either, she disappeared again out to the back and returned in a minute or so with a bright blue plastic pail and a short twig-bundle broom. When Heera saw that her order had been obeyed she gave Ghote one swift venomous look and waddled off up the next flight of stairs, the wooden treads creaking sharply under her weight.

Ghote, standing on guard at the door of the murder room, watched little Munni as she swished water from her pail on to the floor, stooped and with energetic sideways strokes of her broom dealt with the Svashbuckler's mess.

Something in the very liveliness and straightforwardness with which she had set about her not very pleasant task touched a chord in Ghote. He had intended to stand there an impassive sentinel, but instead he spoke.

"The one in there," he said obliquely, nodding his head behind him. "Did I hear you call her Kamla?"

"Yes, she was Kamla."

He heard a choke in the girl's voice and realised that his question had aroused a deeper response in her than might have seemed likely from the coolness she had shown when she had made her gruesome discovery.

"You liked her?" he asked. "She was a particular friend?"

"She—She was my *ma,*" plump little Munni answered, the sound of grief yet clearer in her voice as she continued to wield her broom. "She was the only *ma* I ever had. All I can remember of my child days is sleeping on the footpath wherever it was that I was born, and then one day, just after I had become a woman, you know, I was begging at the railway station there and all of a sudden I thought 'Shall I see where that train goes?' and I hid in it and it came to Bombay. At VT Station a man saw me and said he would take me to somewhere nice. He brought me here and sold me to Heerabai."

She looked up at him, an unexpected glow of pride holding back her looming tears.

"Rupees five hundred he got for me," she said, "because even then I was just the sort of girl men are liking."

"And you began—began the business then?" Ghote asked.

"Yes, yes. I was ready. And I enjoyed. But the best thing was to have Kamla. She was always good to me, a true *ma.*"

And now the tears did come flooding out, bringing with them down her plump cheeks black streaks of the *kohl* with which she had darkened her eyes.

Ghote did not quite know what to do. He put out a hand and hugged the girl's shoulder as she half-squatted, half-knelt in front of him with her broom.

At once she looked up at him, feeling the pressure of his hand on the springy softness of her flesh.

"You want?" she asked. "We cannot go into that room but we can go into one of the others."

"No, no."

He withdrew his comforting hand quickly as if he had accidentally laid it on a sun-scorched rock.

Munni did not seem in any way put out.

"Yes, Kamla was like me," she said. "She was older, of course. Perhaps old enough to be my real *ma.* But she too liked always the business. That is why so many men liked her. You know she was—"

"So many men liked her?" Ghote was unable to prevent himself breaking in. "But do you know who she was with—who she was with when it happened?"

"No," Munni answered, a sudden animal-fierce look drying her tears. "If I did—If I did I would tear out his eyes only with my fingers."

She held up her little hands—the nails were clumsily painted with bright red varnish—and made them into a pair of small claws. But Ghote had no doubt that, pathetic though they looked, she would indeed dart them at the face of any man she knew to have killed her substitute mother and have truly tried to tear out his eyes.

"But do you know anything about the fellow?" he asked.

Now that he had, against his better judgment, begun to do the work that properly belonged to the investigating officer from the nearby Nagpada station—And when was the fellow going to turn up?—he felt he might as well go on with it and hand on any information he gathered.

But again Munni shook her head in negative.

"No, you see," she said, "it was the beginning of the night only. Heerabai had not even finished her bath. I was busy rubbing her with mustard oil the way she likes. So I do not know how that man came. He did not come by the front, I know that. When I saw that Kamla's door was shut already I asked the others down there who she had got, and they said she had taken no one. So it must have been a man who has been here before and knows how to come in by the back."

"There are many like that?" Ghote asked.

"Some. Not many. Some rich ones who are liking us low-caste girls, the ones who want you to have some smell to you, you know, they come in that back way because they are afraid to be seen in a house like this."

Ghote made a mental note to pass on to the officer from the Nagpada station a suggestion to question the house's madam closely about such men. But he doubted very much whether Heera would be helpful. She had nothing to gain and, more than likely, a reputation for discretion to lose.

"But you were going to tell me what your friend Kamla was like," he said to Munni, sensing that the girl would be the happier for talking.

And certainly she looked at once more cheerful.

"Kamla was like me," she said. "To her the business was always fun, even with the men who liked to whip her. She knew how to keep them from doing too much. Until—until—"

The tears looked as if they were going to pour out again.

"But she enjoyed?" Ghote said, putting a little unbelief into his voice so as to provoke a retort that would stave off a new access of grief. "She really enjoyed what she did?"

"But, yes. It's nice, isn't it? Wouldn't you like to be making fun all the time with many, many different girls?"

"Never mind about me," Ghote said quickly. "Tell me about Kamla."

"She was a Kolati girl," Munni answered. "You know in that community when they are old enough they have to choose: will they have a husband or will they go in for prostitution line? And Kamla—she told me often—had seen the *jogtis* walking happily, carrying shining images of gods and goddesses and shouting praises and laughing always, and she knew she wanted to be one of them."

"And when she—when she became one, did it seem as good to her then?"

"Oh, there are some bad days always, but it was better than she thought even. Better, better. She liked and liked and liked."

The words were, as it turned out, a final epitaph for the murdered girl. No sooner had Munni pronounced them, her pretty plump face aglow, than there came the sound of heavy feet on the stairs and the police party from the Nagpada station arrived.

It was led, Ghote saw with a jolt of dismay, by Sub-Inspector D'Silva.

D'Silva, a young Christian officer, had been posted at C.I.D. Headquarters until about a year before and he had not won Ghote's good opinion. A stocky, well-built, swaggering young man who affected the pencil-thin moustache of an airline captain and wore a succession of boldly colourful shirts day after day, he had never hesitated to display his knowledge of the seamier parts of the city, knowledge gained he made tiresomely clear through excessive practical experience. Whether it was because of this or because he invariably cut every corner he could and bullied suspects beyond the limit, he had had a particularly good clear-up rate on the cases that had come his way. So much so that he had soon been posted away to the Nagpada station to take charge of the Vigilante Branch there with its manifold responsibilities for the sexual life of the area, embracing as it did much of notorious Kamatipura.

No, Ghote thought instantly as he recognised that cocky, moustache-embroidered face, if this fellow gets an inkling that someone as rich and with such a high position in society as the Sheriff of Bombay is a suspect in this case there will never be any question of any of it becoming public.

"My God, who have we here?" D'Silva burst out as soon as in the dim light he had spotted Ghote. "Old Ganesh, ace sleuth from Crawford Market. Been up here to sample the wares, have you, Ganeshji? You should have come and seen your old pal first. I could have put you on to some much juicier stuff than these five-rupeewalis."

"I was not here for any such purposes," Ghote answered, more swiftly than he would have liked.

"Oh ho, such morality. You're worse than old D'Sa, *bhai*. And how is my fellow community member? Still going grey with worry about all this modern decadence, eh?"

"D'Sa is very well," Ghote answered. "He is busy with the *bandobust* for the Police Vegetable and Flower Show."

"Well that should keep him out of trouble," D'Silva said. "Until he finds a carrot or a *mooli* root that looks too much like something else."

His laugh resounded clangingly along the narrow passageway.

"Sub-Inspector," Ghote said. "There has been a bad case of murder here. A girl's body very, very horribly mutilated. She is in this room."

"Old Heera lost one of her treasures, has she?" D'Silva replied. "Well, let's see which of the beauties it is."

He barged into the room where Kamla's body lay.

Ghote stood outside in the passageway for a moment, thinking.

Yes. Yes, he would do it. Far from drawing the attention of the investigating officer to the weapon used, he would, if he could, get hold of it himself and whisk it away under the fellow's nose.

That whip was a first-class piece of hard evidence. With any luck it would link the dead girl and the Sheriff of Bombay together so tightly that no amount of courtroom hanky-panky could upset the scientific fact. But let D'Silva get hold of it and it would either disappear entirely or it would go to the Sheriff himself "as a keepsake" in either case for a hefty sum.

He looked into the room. D'Silva was bending over Kamla's body, heaving it over to look at her face.

Ghote stepped quietly forward, reached out to the wall beside him where on the bright-coloured calendar a green-tinged near-naked

Shiva gazed forever amorously at a doe-eyed Parvati, gripped the dangling whip by the very end of its lash far from the fingerprinted handle, twisted the thong once round his fist, jerked the whip off the nails it had rested on and, in one dextrous movement, concealed it behind his back.

He retreated a step to the room's doorway. D'Silva was peering down at the dead girl's face.

"Yeah, Ganesh *bhai,*" he said. "I know this one. She was a goer, man. I've had some spicy fun with her once or twice."

Ghote choked down the reply that had come to his lips.

"Well, Charlie," he said.

Was the fellow's name Charlie? He had never used it before.

"Well, Charlie, I must go off now. I had brought a V.I.P. tourist here and I must be making sure he is quite all right."

"See you, man," D'Silva answered without looking up from the body on the bed.

Ghote slid sideways, still keeping his face towards the open door of the murder room, and then, safely clear, turned and hurried down the rickety stairs leading to the street.

From the corner of his eye he saw little Munni, squatting still with her broom finishing her unsavoury task. She glanced up at him.

Would she make anything of the fact that he had dangling behind his back the whip that had been used to kill her protector and friend? Probably not. What would a girl like that know of fingerprints and police procedures? No, she would forget all about him in a day or two, and soon enough she would carry on unconcerned in the profession which she seemed to get so much unexpected pleasure out of. She would forget him, as in a week or so he would forget her.

In the doorway of the house just before stepping out into the noisy street, half garishly lit from its many barred windows and open shop-fronts, half plunged into dark shadows, he stopped and contrived to stuff the whip underneath his loose shirt without touching its handle. Better that his driver, still waiting at the end of the street, should not see this piece of unorthodoxly obtained evidence. There would be no one in the Fingerprint Bureau at this late hour, but tomorrow first thing he would slip over and have a quiet word with one of the people there he knew.

But next morning when Ghote, having safely deposited the stolen whip with his friend in the Fingerprint Bureau, went to see the A.C.P. matters quickly took a very different course from the one he had expected.

"The Sheriff?" the A.C.P. said when he had heard what Ghote had finally come to suspect at the end of his disastrous visit to Kamatipura with the Svashbuckler. "I don't think that's very likely, Inspector. The fellow was one of India's best-ever cricketers, you know."

"Yes, sir, I am very well knowing. My son was a most keen fan of his batting, sir. He has a picture of him beside his bed still. It is because of that I am sure the man I saw was truly the Rajah of Dhar, Randy Dhar as they are calling him, sir."

The A.C.P. wrinkled his moustache from side to side.

"But you say he was leaving when you arrived?"

"Yes, sir."

"And the passageway in this—this place, it was not very well lit up?"

"No, sir. There was no light there itself."

"Very well then, Ghote, how did you see the fellow?"

"Sir, it was by the light coming through the door of one of the rooms. There are gaps at the top of those doors, sir. They are not all *pukka,* sir. And by a beam of light coming from the furthest of them I saw his face, A.C.P. Sahib."

"No. No, I don't think so, Ghote. Not very likely. Letting your imagination play tricks on you. Not what I like to find in any of my officers."

Ghote stood abashed. He wondered whether to tell the A.C.P. about the whip, that it would possibly prove with scientific certainty that the Sheriff had been in the room where the girl had been murdered. But he was no longer altogether happy about his own conduct over that potentially valuable piece of evidence. He had taken it from the scene of the crime without making sure that his action was witnessed by impartial persons. If the Sheriff was ever brought to court, the fellow's Defence advocates would make chutney out of him over such laxity.

He decided that, especially since he had no way of knowing whether the prints on the whip's handle would indeed correspond with the Sheriff's, he would keep silent about this angle at least for the time being.

"But, sir," he said. "If there is a suspicion only that a person of importance is involved in the matter, sir, shouldn't the case be handled here at Headquarters?"

"Not at all, Ghote, not at all. You say Sub-Inspector D'Silva is in charge from Nagpada? Well, I have seen his Service Sheet and I am very well satisfied with it. An officer with an excellent record, Inspector. Likely to go far."

"Yes, sir."

Ghote stood in silence for a moment. He knew really that the interview had come to an end. The A.C.P. had taken one of his shiny brass paperweights off the pile of papers it was protecting from the breeze of his desk fan and had put it down on the dark surface of his desk. He could scarcely have given a clearer indication that important work awaited.

"But, sir," Ghote burst out nevertheless. "Sir, if you had seen those marks on the body, sir, and the way that whip had been pulled round the girl's neck. It was the work of a maniac only, sir. Sir, should it be that the man is not after all just someone who can be picked up in the red-light area, then he is a great, great danger to the public, sir."

"To the public, Ghote? Well, you can call it the public if you like. But the fellow, even if he wasn't some local *dada* taking revenge on a girl who had stepped out of line, is obviously going to confine his activities to the prostitute class. I don't think it's a matter that need worry us at Headquarters. Dismiss, Inspector."

"Yes, sir. Yes, A.C.P. Sahib."

Ghote clicked his heels, turned and marched out of the A.C.P.'s big, airy office. A miserable man.

5

Back at his desk, confronting once more the case of the major general's son and the stolen platinum chain, Inspector Ghote found the notes he had made from the fat tome in Records of all known chain-snatching and cinema-ticket fraud criminals hard going. Which one of them would be worth chasing up in whatever unsavoury part of Bombay he was recorded as living in? Would a trip to somewhere in the not too distant *mofussil*, the noted native-place of some particular gang member, be worth the time and effort?

Would it be possible somehow to get hold of the fingerprints of the Sheriff of Bombay and—

No. He was working on the City Light Cinema chain-snatching. That and nothing else.

He forced himself to read on.

Zinabhai Darji, aged 26, convicted at Esplanade Police Court of attempting to snatch one gold chain at or near Mahala-mi Temple, sentenced to one month's rigorous imprisonment. . . . Native-place: Mehsana, Gujarat.

No. A not very courageous Gujarati, probably making his sole attempt at theft. Certainly not worth going all the way out there on the chance he had gone home following a more successful try.

After all, dammit, the A.C.P. could not have been more clear. The Falkland Road murder was to be strictly for the Nagpada station to handle. It was chance only that he himself had been on the scene. Double chance that he had glimpsed that face. So, forget.

Forget, forget, forget.

Kanchan Phaterphaker, aged 23, convicted at Ballard Pier Police Court of snatching a gold chain. Sentenced to six months R.I. . . .

Very doubtful. Someone working the bus queues in the dockland area was not going to be a member of a gang operating on Matunga side, eight or nine miles away and a district of a completely different character.

But that face which it was such double chance to have glimpsed: it was the Sheriff of Bombay's. It was. It was. And if it was, if the Sheriff had committed that frenzied, madman's murder, was he not one day, sooner or later, going to do the same thing again?

No, he had said all that to the A.C.P. and the A.C.P. had been quite plain in his answer. "Dismiss, Inspector," he had said. No business of yours. No business of ours at Headquarters. We have quite enough on our hands without that. We have the City Light Cinema chain-snatching case.

Ghote pushed himself to his feet and set off once again for the narrow, rubbish-strewn lane in Matunga where, just a fortnight earlier, a young man willing to pay twenty rupees for a ten-rupee best seat had lost a platinum chain valued at rupees six thousand, and where perhaps a witness was still to be found.

But that evening, back at home, he was not able to expel from his mind the thought of the prostitute Kamla and what little, plump, happy Munni had told him about her. Of what he had learnt, and of how he had seen the dead girl lying on the bed—its dull blue-checked bedcover had been rucked up at one corner to reveal a thin greyed stripy mattress—her head savagely wrenched to one side by the violence with which in the end she had been strangled.

"What for are you sitting and standing and sitting again all the time?"

He looked up from the thoughts that had taken him back once more to the noise and the crowds and the blatant sexual marketing of Falkland Road.

His wife was standing staring down at him, an expression of considerable exasperation on her face.

"It is nothing, nothing."

"Five minutes past I was asking if you were wanting a *paan.* You still have not answered yes or no."

"Oh yes. Yes. That is, no. No, I do not want any *paan.*"

"When I have made only?"

Furiously Protima thrust out her hand in which there lay the spice-packed, bright green, neat triangle of folded betel leaf cunningly secured with a clove. A symbol of wifely duty, however little tendered at this moment with wifely humility.

"Oh yes. Yes, I will take. Your *paans* are always so good."

He took the folded leaf, thrust it into his mouth and chewed with vigorous appreciation.

For perhaps five up and down jaw movements.

Should he talk about his problem to Protima? It was his principle not to discuss police affairs outside of office. But then again on the other hand sometimes he had let that principle go hang. And sometimes even what Protima had said to him had been helpful. She never understood anything about what police work really meant, of course. But sometimes something she had said, had, it was true, somehow made him see something in a different light.

But to mention the Sheriff of Bombay. To say out loud that it was possible that someone as respected as the Sheriff of Bombay had at about 1830 hours the previous evening brutally murdered one Kamla, a prostitute, in the notorious Cages? No, no. That could not be done.

That was something to keep in his own head only, until he had proof-proof that it was true. No one, not even a wife who had never gossiped away a single one of his secrets, must ever know what he had seen. Not now that he had reported the matter to his superior officer and been told that he had not seen what he had.

But he had.

"Now, what for are you pacing and pacing the room?"

He looked round. It was true he was on his feet again. And he had been sitting down. Chewing a *paan*.

He found to his dismay that the whole little bundle was still almost intact in his cheek.

He slunk back to his chair, placed himself in it in an attitude of complete repose and chewed and chewed and chewed.

And then he realised, something he ought to have seen long before, perhaps as soon as he had set foot inside the door, that he was not the only one with something on his mind. Protima, too, was distressed.

Her unease had expressed itself differently from his. Where he had not been able to stop himself moving about she had lost all her customary gracefulness of movement. The flowing rightness that she had always possessed even in the least little action, adjusting the collar of young Ved's shirt, keeping her own sari draped to its best advantage, lifting the bundle of tamarind leaves she kept in the food cupboard for freshness to take something out from behind it, all had vanished. Instead she was stiff and tense, and unusually silent.

"But, you," he said, "what for are you worrying? Are you ill? Some fever? Or Ved? Ved, is he ill just now?"

Protima turned and stood facing him. And, yes, her body was rigid as a crippled beggar's crutch-pole.

"Do you think everything-everything can be put down to symptoms only?" she broke out. "Do you think everything that goes wrong with a person is no more than some fever that will go away before long?"

"But—But—But it is not fever that Ved has got? That you have got?"

Ghote felt his every bearing had suddenly been twisted round.

"Fever? Fever only? I tell you that boy has got worse-worse than fever. His mind is sick. Sick, sick, sick. His mind is sunk in deepest filth, and all you do is talk about fever."

"In filth? What filth? Ved's mind is sick? What only are you saying?"

Protima's eyes flashed with a fire that had been for too many hours kept in check.

"I am saying?" she shot back at him. "Now you are making out that it is all in my head only. But you would not get away with it so easily. I have proof. Proof-proof I have got."

She left the room in a banner-streaming flutter of flying sari.

Ghote sat rooted to his chair, wondering how exactly it had come about that suddenly he was engulfed in such a tempest of accusations, of accusations of he knew not what. And something else was trying to obtrude into his dazed and disoriented mind.

Proof-proof, Protima had said that she had. Of something? Of whatever it was. And it was proof-proof that he had been worrying over before all this had so abruptly cascaded down on to him. Proof-proof that the Sheriff of Bombay was a frenzied sex killer, a dangerous maniac beneath the happy exterior of the glossy photographs that were to be seen, jostling with those of film stars, saints, gods and goddesses, in half the picture stalls of Bombay. And one even pinned up beside Ved's bed.

Pinned up beside Ved's bed. A glossy photograph of the Rajah of Dhar, Randy Dhar, former hero Indian cricketer, now Sheriff of Bombay.

And a glossy photograph, it was well known, was an ideal surface to take fingerprints. Indeed, you had to be careful handling photographs for just that reason. So . . . So would it not be possible, daring but possible, to borrow Ved's photo, clean its surface with the utmost care and then take it to the Sheriff and ask him to sign it "for my son"?

Then . . . Then that glossy sheet would have the Sheriff's fingerprints, as he held it down to write on it, stamped clearly as if his hand had been pressed on to an ink pad and then transferred to one of Records cardboard sheets to be inserted in the flapping file machine that was their pride and joy. After that, easy enough to take the photo round to Karadkar in the Fingerprint Bureau and get it checked against the prints that were bound to be on the smooth leather of the whip which had been used to strangle poor wretched Kamla. And then he would have, surely, proof.

"Here, look. Proof-proof."

Coming back to reality from this new reverie he somehow expected to find Protima offering him the photograph of the Sheriff, the daring shaven Sikh heedless of the dictates of the religion of his birth about uncut hair, face bare even to a moustache and all the more dashingly handsome for that, eyes twinkling merrily beneath the deep-peaked India cricket cap, teeth showing white and confident in a lazy, easy smile. The face he had seen, clearly and beyond doubt, in the brothel in Falkland Road.

But, instead, Protima was pushing towards him a thin, cheap-looking book with, muzzily reproduced in lurid colours on its paper cover, a picture of an almost naked Western woman presenting her backside foremost. The title of this surprising affair was apparently *Janus,* and as he peered more closely he realised that it was a smearily reproduced copy of some English sex magazine. The price in English money could just be made out at the top corner, overstamped in purple ink with *Rs 5*.

"What—What for are you showing me this?" he asked, as unwillingly he took the wretched production into his hands.

"What for am I showing it?" Protima answered, her voice filled with maternal fury. "Because I am finding it hidden under some loose tiles behind Ved's bed only."

Ghote experienced a sense of shock. At once to realise that it had sprung not from horror that a son of his should have been reading whatever the magazine *Janus* had offered long ago for the titillation of its Western readers but—perhaps it was more a topsy-turvying surprise than a shock—from finding that Ved was now, suddenly, of an age to be engrossed by naked women. And it had seemed only yesterday that he was still being nursed at Protima's breast and was struggling even to walk.

But then he recalled, not without some little internal arithmetic, that Ved was actually now thirteen years of age. And next, with an abrupt lurch of dismay, he remembered that some of the prostitutes he had seen the night before in Falkland Road could not have been much older and that from what plump little Munni had told him of herself she had cheerfully begun in "the business" at that age.

"Well," he said cautiously, opening the book's rough-paper pages. "Well, you know, boys will be boys. It is natural for a young man to think about women, you know. We must remember little Ved is growing up."

"Natural? Natural for my son to think such dirty thoughts as that?"

Protima directed a long, thin, beautifully elegant finger down towards the magazine Ghote was holding. The scorn that jetted from its tip ought to have shrivelled the wretched thing into instant ashes.

But it had not.

"You have looked inside?" Ghote asked. "It is very debauched?"

"What do you think I am?" Protima turned her wrath fully on to him now. "Am I a prostitute only that I should look at such things? One glance at the outside was enough. More than enough. The shameless, shameless woman."

"Yes. Yes, very bad," Ghote felt able to agree. "A very fourth-class woman altogether."

But he remembered the almost equally bare backsides that had been happily flicked at him and the Svashbuckler as they had entered Falkland Road the evening before, and somehow, without being able exactly to define how, he felt that they had not altogether belonged to very, very fourth-class women.

He looked down at the opened magazine.

And, to his complete surprise and rapidly growing amusement, he saw that what was printed on its coarse pages bore no relation to what had been crudely colour-daubed on the cover. The contents were, he discovered as he looked more closely, nothing other than something called *The All-India Boys and Girls Book of Facts,* a higgledy-piggledy assortment of possibly useful general knowledge items.

"But, listen," he said to Protima, "listen to what poor Ved has coughed out rupees five to buy wrapped up in see-through paper. *Question: What does Y.M.C.A. stand for? Answer:*—and not exactly a likely answer really—*Young Women's Christian Association.* Well, if you did not know that unlikely fact, Ved now does. And here is something else. *What is stenography? Answer: The science of bodies or forces at rest or in equilibrium."*

He could no longer keep back the laughter.

"Poor, poor Ved," he said, tears beginning to run down his cheeks. "All that money paid out, all that much of excitements promised, and what is he getting? A book of facts with most of them not true facts even. What a trick. What a bluff for the poor boy."

A piece of paper fluttered down from the laughter-shaken pages of the transformed sex book. Ghote picked it up and looked at it, blinking away the tears in his eyes. It was a cutting from a newspaper, an advertisement boldly headed "For Married Persons Only" of a book entitled *Mysteries of Marriage—Latest Revised Edition With 40 Intimate Illustrations.* At the foot of the text there was a boxed-off "Declaration of Oath" reading "I hereby solemnly declare on oath that I am a married person of major age . . ." And where there was a space, very small, for "True Signature" Ved had written, with plainly shaking hand, his name.

"But he has not sent it off," Ghote said, handing the slip to Protima.

"And he will not," she answered, crumpling it in an instant. "And this I would burn also," she added, seizing the lurid *Book of Facts.*

"Well, yes, if you like," Ghote said. "I expect Ved has forgotten he hid it where he did, forgotten that you pull out his whole bed sometimes."

"Forgotten this?" Protima said, shaking the poor innocent *Book of Facts* as if it were swarming with white ants. "How would he forget something that looks so disgusting?"

"Well, we would see. But I remember when I was a boy or young man and we had first shifted to Bombay I bought two-three dirty pictures and hid them somewhere outside so that my parents would not find. But in the end I could not exactly remember where I had put. Perhaps they are there still even, in some crevice in a tree in Shivaji Park near where we first stayed."

This intimate revelation seemed to impress Protima more than any of his earlier authoritative assertions. Her rigidity of stance melted away, and she looked at him for the first time that evening with sympathy.

"And you are thinking that Ved has the same feelings also?" she asked. "That he was interested in this terrible picture on the front of the book for a little while only?"

Ghote wagged his head.

"Who can tell?" he said. "Perhaps the boy was more-more interested than I was at his age. But it is likely also that he was not, that he bought the book when some of his friends put him up to it with a bet and then he became more keen on cricket once again."

"Yes. Yes, that may be so."

Protima looked happier. She put a long-fingered hand up to the *pallu* of her sari and twitched it slightly into more becoming folds.

But the mention of cricket had rewoken Ghote's mind to his own preoccupation. He found now, however, that somehow he was able to put before Protima the dilemma he had previously felt he must confront alone.

"But there is something I have to tell for myself," he said.

"Yes? Yes, what is it?"

And to Protima's growingly anxious concern, in a few brief sentences he unravelled the whole of his complexity.

"And the A.C.P. Sahib ordered that you would do nothing?" she asked at the end of his recital.

"Yes. Dismiss, Inspector, he was saying. Dismiss."

Protima stood looking down at him thoughtfully. Ghote felt a blessed sense of relief that at least now there was someone who was in tune with his difficulty to the full.

He told her what he thought might be done with Ved's photo of the hero cricketer.

"Yes, yes. That at least you must do. Then if they cannot find that man's fingerprints on—on that terrible thing that was used, then your trouble will be over."

"Yes. Yes."

It was a wonderful prospect.

"But," Protima said suddenly, "in what way can you get to see that man, get to the Sheriff, such a *bahadur* as he is, such a posh fellow."

"Oh, I will go to him," Ghote answered. "I will find some reason and go, and then I will say, 'Oh, Sheriff Sahib, my son is a very, very great admirer, may please I have autograph?'"

But inwardly he realised that reaching the moment of making that polite request would not perhaps be as simple as he had indicated. To get to see a man like the Sheriff of Bombay: in itself that would be not at all an easy business.

Yet he allowed himself to bask in the look of admiration that Protima gave him and said nothing. A moment later they heard Ved's careless, jumping steps outside and Protima hurried away to put the double-faced magazine she had found out of sight until she could destroy it.

All next day Ghote contrived, when he had any time to himself, to continue to glow from that moment of wifely awe, even though he was unable immediately to devise any reasonable way in which a simple Inspector of the Bombay Police could get to see as treetops-treading a figure as the Sheriff of Bombay.

It was a problem that continued to go without an answer for several days more, and in the evening there were increasingly difficult inquiries to fend off from Protima and from Ved, promised a signature to his picture. But Ghote consoled himself with the thought that, even if the Sheriff was the sex killer who had dealt so horribly with Kamla, it was not likely that the terrible impulse would visit him again at once.

But then one morning, just after he had settled in his cabin and was reaching into his desk drawer to pull out the last few of his notes on Bombay's chain-snatchers, his bugbear of old, Inspector D'Sa, thrust his lean grey head over the bat-wing doors of the cabin.

"Ah, young Ghote. Not busy, I see. When I was first in the force we used to be hard at work long before this hour."

"Well, I am just beginning."

Ghote thumped his bundle of notes squarely in front of himself on the glass-topped surface of his desk. But D'Sa, as he had known would be the case, took no notice but pushed open the doors and entered.

"Well, man," he said in as relaxed a conversational tone as his rigid manner permitted, "have you heard the news?"

Ghote sighed and looked up.

"No, Inspector, what news is it?"

"Another sex murder in our city. In Nagpada. They wanted to know if we were interested since the victim is at least middle class, a student from the university. But A.C.P. Sahib was damn firm about it. Nagpada crime, he said, Nagpada investigation. Quite right."

But in Ghote's mind a fearful deep black hole was opening every moment more and more widely.

"Sex murder?" he said, swallowing. "What sort of sex murder?"

"Oh, the girl was beaten with a whip. But I tell you, Ghote, it is one sign more only of what is going on in this city. Degeneration, darkness and obscenity. That is what it is. Degeneration, darkness and obscenity."

6

The pattern was all too familiar. Ghote, sitting at his desk, his scrawled notes of chain-snatchers in front of him, Inspector D'Sa grizzled and upright peering down at him, saw again with awful vividness the body of the prostitute Kamla lying on the low bed in the Falkland Road brothel, the corner of its dull blue-checked cloth rucked back to show the thin greyed stripy mattress below.

No, there could be no shuffling away from it. The man who had so brutally killed Kamla had plainly already given way again to his appalling impulse and had taken another life. And that man was in terrible likelihood the Sheriff of Bombay, the person he himself had seen being smuggled out of the Falkland Road brothel only minutes before Kamla's body had been found.

Inwardly he cursed himself. He had the means of proving that man was Kamla's killer. He had the photograph of that smiling, confident, clean-shaven, twinkling-eyed hero, taken from its place beside Ved's bed and carefully polished free of any lingering finger impressions. At this moment it was in the bottommost drawer of his desk, underneath the towel he kept there to wipe his face with when the heat was at its worst. He could have gone to see the Sheriff and worked his simple trick on him with it at any time in the last ten days.

And he had done nothing.

And now another girl was dead, strangled. Whipped and strangled. When, had he acted as he should have done, as he had pledged himself to Protima to do, he might have been able in all good time to take to the A.C.P. scientific proof. And the Sheriff of Bombay, maniac killer, would have been safely behind bars.

But there was nothing for it now save to act at once. This very day somehow. This very morning. At this very hour.

Inspector D'Sa was grumbling on still. He had not heard a word of it.

"Sorry, D'Sa Sahib, you were saying?"

"You see, it is a question, Ghote, of getting a first-class V.V.I.P."

"A first-class V.V.I.P.? Of getting him?"

Did D'Sa, too, know who the maniac killer was? Was he, too, as much at a loss about how to bring such a figure to justice?

"Yes, yes. Are you listening even, Ghote? God knows, it is trouble enough to put up a good effort for the show without having no one willing to listen to what I am telling them."

The show? What show?

And then it dawned on him. He looked up at the grizzled inspector with sudden delight.

"You are wanting a V.V.I.P. to open the Police Vegetable and Flower Show?" he asked.

"What else have I been saying for the past five minutes? You young officers, you think of nothing but your own affairs day and night. No esprit de corps. No esprit de corps at all. When I was a young—"

"Inspector, what about asking the Sheriff to open your show?"

"The Sheriff? The Sheriff of Bombay?"

"Well, yes. Isn't he a first-class fellow to do it?"

"Yes. Yes, Inspector, he would be. But . . . But I do not know whether I could go up to a gentleman like that and ask."

"But I would do it for you, D'Sa Sahib. It would be a pleasure to me only."

"You would?"

"I would. I would go now. Now, this very instant. And I tell you something else. I have got a photo of the fellow here in my desk, belonging to my son. I would take it and get his signed autograph on it."

"Ah. Now I see. This is what you were wanting all the time. You young officers, it is self, self with you."

The Rajah of Dhar, Sheriff of Bombay, lived still in the huge house on Malabar Hill that had been his family's Bombay residence for nearly a century, though, walking up to it jittering with inward doubts, Ghote was able to observe that it was far from being nowadays in a state of good repair. From the closed shutters at the far ends of its imposing grey walls it looked indeed as if large parts of it were out of use altogether. But nevertheless it was one of the few remaining houses of all the huge residences, now replaced by towering apartment blocks, that had once, each in its own secluded grounds, occupied this most salubrious area of Bombay, saved from the worst steaminess of the city's weather by the height and the breezes off the sea below.

Yes, Ghote thought, queasiness flickering more violently in his stomach, the fellow still must have plenty of money even though the former state rulers' privy purses have been suppressed and their titles officially taken away.

Yet whoever called the man he was going to accost plain Mr. Randhir Singh? No, the fellow continued to use the name Rajah of Dhar, and everybody was delighted to kowtow to that.

He tapped the briefcase dangling at his side to reassure himself that in it there was the simple means by which such a giant, such a figure from the highest world, could be caught. Could be shown up for what he was, a maniac killer.

There were four wide steps leading up to the tall front door of the house. Beside the door there was a bell-push, in brass, well polished still, glinting in the sun.

Ghote swallowed once, clumped up the steps, one, two, three, four, put out a hand as if it belonged to someone else, some figure in a film, and pressed the bell-button. Away, far away inside the big house he thought he could hear a jangling sound.

No going back now.

He waited. The sun, striking the back of his neck above his shirt collar, brought up a prickle of sweat despite the winter season.

The door in front of him swung open. A bearer, tall, white-uniformed, wearing an elaborate pink turban, stood there.

Ghote swallowed again, and handed him his card.

"To see the Sheriff Sahib," he said. "On behalf of the Commissioner of Police."

He felt a small inner sense of triumph. These were the words he had promised himself he would say, and he had said them. He was not going to call the fellow Rajah of Dhar. And he had not done. He was going, as he had a right to do, to use the name of the Commissioner when it was a matter concerning the whole Bombay force that he was here to discuss. And he had done so.

"Please, come," the soldier-tall, pink-turbaned servant said.

He led Ghote into a high, marble-paved hall. Its walls were decorated with soaring white pillars. Between them on plinths of various colours there were chill white statues, seemingly all of Western subjects. There was a little girl holding an open umbrella. There was a sprawling fat baby. There were several naked maidens modestly clutching formless garments between their half-bent legs. Through wide doorways glimpses were to be had of large rooms to either side. One had two billiard tables in it, shrouded under covers. Another boasted an enormous dining table running its full length and capable of seating, Ghote calculated rapidly, as many as fifty people.

The bearer left him in a room mercifully smaller, though it was large enough and filled formidably with various pieces of European furniture, heavy armchairs stiffly upholstered, glass-fronted cabinets containing little vases and objects in silver and china, small tables here and there with silver-framed photographs on them.

"Rajah Sahib is having meeting," the bearer said. "He may come after some time."

"Yes," Ghote answered.

He went over and sat himself down in one of the large chairs, as if nothing was more natural to him. The bearer left. Ghote got up again. He wished the fellow had shut the door so that he could feel at ease being ill at ease. But it had been left firmly ajar and he did not dare do anything about it.

Time slowly passed.

Ghote began to wish that he had telephoned and made an appointment. He had thought of doing so. But then he had been struck by the notion that, if the Sheriff had only the night before committed his terrible crime once again, he might very well not agree to any policewalla of any sort coming to see him.

The fellow might, of course, even now take fright when the bearer handed him his card and leave the huge house by any one of countless ways out. But if he did, it would surely be an admission of guilt.

Nevertheless Ghote went and placed himself as near the room's open door as he decently could. If the Rajah elected to leave by the front he would see him. And then . . . ?

Well, leave that to what happened when it did.

Eventually, however, he got tired of standing peering out while still trying not to let any servant who might pass by see him. He retreated again, but was unable to bring himself to sit. He began examining the photographs on the table nearest him. One was of the then Prince of Wales standing with the present Rajah's grandfather.

With an inner thud of doom, Ghote realised that he knew something about that dated-looking bearded and turbaned figure. He had been notorious. Notoriously sex-obsessed. An out-and-out sadist. His history was revived from time to time in the cheaper newspapers. He had had eventually to quit his *gaddi* after pressure from the viceroy. He had burnt alive a polo pony which had failed him in the field, and that had been the last straw for the British. But there had been whispers of other brutal deaths earlier, of dancing girls, of young boys.

Suddenly from outside there was the sound of voices. People were coming down the wide flight of stairs not far from where he was. The voices were loud, confident and cheerful. And talking in English.

"A most successful meeting."

"Yes, yes."

"Rajah Sahib, let me thank you again for letting us come to your beautiful house."

So he was there. The Rajah. The Sheriff of Bombay. The probable sex killer.

"Not at all, not at all."

That was his voice, the man's voice. Just like a real Englishman's, like a donkey braying only.

Would he ever manage to make that request to him, "Oh, Sheriff Sahib, my son is a very, very great admirer . . ."?

"Not at all, not at all. The All-India Social Hygiene Samaj does such important work, it is the least I could do to invite you to hold a meeting here."

The All-India Social Hygiene Samaj. Surely that was the organisation devoted to considering the problem of prostitution? And the fellow had invited them to meet in his own house. The slayer of Kamla the prostitute had done that. If he had, what daring he had shown. What colossal cheek.

But perhaps, after all, he was not that slayer. Yet he had been there at the Falkland Road brothel at the time of the killing. He had been. With his own eyes he had seen him. Beyond any possibility of doubt.

So that means of proof he possessed must be used. It must. He must, come what may, get that photograph signed.

The committee members of the Samaj trooped on towards the door, the Sheriff's voice loud in farewells.

But two of the party, evidently, had dropped behind. They were standing just outside. Two women. Ghote could hear their lowered voices easily. In his mind's eye he could see the pair of them, matronly, bulging with good feeding, wearing nine-yard silk saris, the ones that came right down to the ground and had to be changed twice a day because of the dirt they picked up.

The voices were quiet and confidential. But he could still make out every word.

"So, my dear, now you've seen Randy Dhar, what do you think of our modern Krishna?"

"Well, my dear, he certainly is every bit as handsome in the flesh as in those magazine photographs. No wonder our Krishna has all those *gopis* in love with him."

A laugh, which had it not issued from a matronly person would have been a schoolgirl giggle.

"And are you going to join the ranks of the milkmaids now, become yet another *gopi?*"

"No, certainly not. I admit, if I had not heard all the scandals about his promiscuous life, I would have been charmed with him. His smile only would have done that. But, when I am knowing what I do, I felt only a revulsion."

"Well, yes. Yes, my dear, I understand that. He is . . . Well, he is what he is. But all the same . . ."

"No. A revuls—"

"Sssh, my dear."

"Oh, Rajah Sahib, may I thank you once again? A so successful meeting."

"Not at all, not at all, ladies. But now, if you'll excuse me, I have someone waiting to see me."

Ghote, too near the other side of the door, stepped hastily backwards, bumped into the table with the photograph of the late Prince of Wales on it, managed just to stop it toppling over, straightened from holding it, his body all damp with sweat, and found himself face to face with the Sheriff of Bombay.

"It is—" The Sheriff glanced down at the little piece of pasteboard in his hand. "Inspector Ghote?"

"Yes, yes. Raj—Yes, Sheriff Sahib."

"Well, and what can I do for you, Inspector? Not come to arrest me, I suppose?"

The eyes that twinkled perpetually in Ved's glossy photograph twinkled yet more in real life now, and the man himself was even more impressive in a beautifully cut wool suit with a striped tie in heavy silk decorating a shirt white and wide as a ship's sail.

"No. No, no."

"Well, my dear fellow, I didn't really expect that, you know. When I am arrested I dare say Commissioner Sahib will come to do it himself."

Yes, Ghote thought. Yes, it will come to that, I suppose. The Commissioner, or at least the A.C.P., Crime Branch. When he had taken to them the report from the Fingerprint Bureau. If in the end he could get himself to the point of playing his trick on this man, this suited and booted descendant of a notorious grandfather.

"Inspector?"

The Rajah's voice had just an edge of sharpness. Ghote, a flood of sweat now springing up all over him, realised that he had been standing in dumbstruck silence. What—What was it that he had been asked?

"I—I am sorry, Sheriff Sahib."

"Well, no doubt you are, my dear fellow. But unless you have the kindness to tell me what it is you want I shan't actually be able to do anything for you."

"Oh. No. No, I see. It is a phot—No. It is the Vegetable and Flower Show."

"Ah, ha. And you want me to grow a cauliflower as big as a beach ball for this event, wherever it is?"

"No, no, no, no, Sheriff Sahib. It is the Police Vegetable and Flower Show. The annual Police Vegetable and Flower Show."

"Ah, the annual show, that makes a difference of course."

Ghote swallowed.

What difference did that make? What was the fellow talking about? And Ved's photo? Could he ask that favour now?

Then, suddenly, he realised. It had been some sort of a joke, the business of it making a difference. Yes, a sort of joke. But too late to laugh now.

"No, no, Sheriff Sahib. I am sorry, I am altogether forgetting to ask you what it is exactly I came to request. It is opening the show. Sheriff Sahib, would you do us the very great honour to open our show?"

"Well, yes, my dear fellow. What is a Sheriff for, after all, but to open shows, or to close them, or whatever?"

"To close the show, Sheriff Sahib? But I am thinking it is usual only to have our show opened."

"Exactly, my dear chap. Then I'll open it. If I can. But, you see, you've omitted to tell me when this doubtless delightful event takes place."

"Takes place? Oh. Oh yes, the date. The date."

Ghote scrabbled in his mind. When the hell had D'Sa said the wretched affair was to be?

At last a date floated to the surface. Was it the right one? Well, no matter.

"It is December the twentieth, Sheriff Sahib."

"Ah. Well, at that time I do have a deuce of a lot on. I'll have to have a look-see in my diary. Come with me to my den, my dear fellow, and we'll sort it all out in a jiffy."

The Sheriff led him up the sweeping marble stairs, along a wide corridor lined with broad rosewood doors and into one of the rooms off it. This was evidently his private place. It was not large but had an air of extreme comfort. There were only two armchairs, cane-seated and cane-backed for coolness, and a divan against the far wall. Besides these there was a tall old desk with its roll top pushed back to disclose a mass of papers and an ornate bookcase. Ghote, waiting while the Sheriff flipped through a large leather-bound diary, was unable to read any of the titles behind the glass front of this last, except that he thought he recognised a recent illustrated edition of the *Kama Sutra* which had caused something of a sensation on its first appearance because it had been priced at the daunting sum of eight hundred rupees.

But, immediately above the impressively ornate bookcase, there was something that was startlingly easy to read. Hanging against the darkly papered wall, blatantly incongruous, there was a crudely painted notice. It must date, Ghote thought, from the time of Mrs. Gandhi's Emergency. It read *Fight Immorals*.

"Ah, I see you like my little trophy," the Sheriff said, suddenly glancing up from the diary. "Pinched from somewhere in my unregenerate days, I'm afraid. The aftermath of some post-match celebration. I think we must have won by an inning or something, and I suppose I ought not to hang on to it now I've become so respectable."

Ghote was aware, all too aware, that he was being looked down on. The Sheriff was tall and stood easily upright. Easily and with the careless glance of utter confidence.

"Or now that," he added, with an extra twinkle in his eyes, "I am meant to be respectable."

"Oh yes, Sheriff Sahib."

Ghote had not known at all what to reply.

The Sheriff smiled. Even white teeth flashing.

"But between men of the world like you and I, Inspector, there can't be too much pretence, can there?"

"Oh no. No, Sheriff Sahib."

"So . . . So I can safely admit to all sorts of naughty goings-on, eh? To all those ladies who will insist that I bed them? To not being your Lakshman never looking at Sita above her feet? To all sorts of things, hm?"

"No. Yes. Yes, Sheriff Sahib, I am very well understanding."

What else could I have answered, Ghote thought desperately. And how can I get the subject back to cricket? To cricket and my son's very, very great admiration? And what the fellow is saying makes it all the more important to get that scientific proof. He is boasting. Boasting of the women he has at his mercy, of his many conquests. He is nearly proclaiming himself to be the killer of those two girls.

"Well now," the Sheriff said in a more briskly businesslike tone, "what was that date again?"

What was it? What was it?

"It was—It was December the thirtieth, Sheriff Sahib."

"Oh? I thought you said the twentieth. I know I'm particularly booked up just before Christmas."

"Yes, yes. The twentieth. It was the twentieth I was meaning. Most sorry, Sheriff Sahib."

"So long as you've got it right now, old chap."

Casually the Sheriff went on flicking through the leather-bound, gold-edged diary.

"Yes, Sheriff Sahib. It is the twentieth, I am sure of that now."

Was it? But did it matter? Before the opening of the Vegetable and Flower Show would not the Sheriff of Bombay, self-confessed lecher, be in a cell awaiting trial?

Provided that vital fingerprint evidence was there to be used . . .

"Sheriff Sahib, there is something else also. It is my son, Sheriff Sahib. He is a very—"

"Ah, here we are. The twentieth. Absolutely clear in the afternoon. Afternoon suit you, Inspector?"

"Afternoon?"

"For me to do my stuff, opening your thingummy? Always delighted to back up the police, you know. Greatest respect for all you chaps."

"Oh yes. The afternoon would be a very good time. Thank you."

"Then shall we say three o'clock? About right, eh?"

"Yes, yes. Three o'clock. We are most grateful, Sheriff Sahib. The Commissioner . . ."

"Yes, yes. Fine. Well, thank you, my dear chap, for asking me. And now, if you'll excuse me, I have a certain lady I should be phoning. My dear fellow, a pair of breasts that ought to be kept in a museum. So I dare say you can find your own way out. By clever detective work, eh?"

"Yes. Yes, of course, Sheriff Sahib."

Ghote found himself turning and walking towards the broad rosewood door.

He stopped. Swung round. Brought up his briefcase, fumbled with its catches.

"Please," he said. "Please. My son. Very, very great admiration. Please."

He had got the photograph out—thank goodness he had contrived to hold it by its edge—and thrust it dartingly now at the Sheriff, as if he was a pickpocket's accomplice set on distracting a fat-looking tourist by his importuning.

The Sheriff looked down at what he was holding.

A wide smile lit up his face.

"The well-known features," he said. "And an autograph, I suppose? My pleasure entirely, Inspector."

He cleared a space on his desk, laid the glossy photograph on it and placing his hand fairly and squarely down to hold it in place prepared to write.

"Did I hear you say for your son?"

"Yes, yes, Sheriff Sahib."

Briefly Ghote thought of Ved, of his simple desire to have this trophy made doubly valuable, of his little shameful secret that had been hidden underneath his bed.

"So, what's the lad's name?"

"It is Ved, Sheriff Sahib. Ved."

"Good. And he's a cricketer, is he?"

"Oh yes, Sheriff Sahib. A most keen cricketer."

"Fine."

And the Sheriff of Bombay wrote with a great flourish on the shiny, fingerprint-taking surface all across his own smiling, self-confident features.

It was less than an hour later that Ghote looked up from the blinding square of white light in the darkness of the Fingerprint Bureau.

"You are sure?" he asked.

"One hundred percent, Ganesh *bhai*. The prints on this picture— *To young Ved. Keep a straight bat. Randhir Singh Dhar.* That is very nice—are one and the same as the set on that beautifully smooth whip that you were bringing me. One and the same, no possible doubt about it."

7

The A.C.P. took the two photographs of sets of fingerprints and tossed them to one side of his sweeping semicircular desk.

"Yes, yes," he said. "That is all very well, Ghote. But I am not going to go to court with this only."

"But, sir. But, A.C.P. Sahib. But this is one hundred percent proof, sir. That fellow was at—"

"Fellow? Fellow? Who are you speaking about, Inspector?"

The A.C.P.'s head had snapped up like a puppet's suddenly jerked by a puppet-master above.

"I mean the Sheriff, sir. The Rajah of Dhar, sir."

"Well, well, no need to give him a title that has been officially abolished, man. No need for that sort of thing at all."

"No, sir. But, sir, it nevertheless remains that the Sheriff was in that room, sir, that he was using the whip that strangled that prostitute, Kamla. We have proof of that, sir. Proof that no one can challenge."

"No, Inspector? You think not?"

Ghote looked at the A.C.P. across the wide desk. There could be no mistaking the sharpness of the gaze that looked back at him.

"Sir, I am thinking it," he said, finding his voice trailing miserably away despite the belief he had striven to put into it.

"But you are not thinking enough, Ghote. You yourself told me how that whip got to Fingerprint Bureau. You took it there with your own hands. With your own hands, and with no witnesses. You have no witnesses that the whip which they took the prints from was one and the same whip that was in that Falkland Road brothel. What is a Defence advocate going to make of that, do you think?"

"Yes, sir, it is true," Ghote said.

He had been aware of this fault in the case against the Sheriff from the very outset. But somehow, with his triumph in getting hold of a guaranteed set of the man's prints on Ved's photo, he had succeeded in pushing the thought of this weakness to some distant recess of his mind. Now it stared at him blatantly as a film hoarding.

"No, no, Ghote. Up to now we have no case at all, no case at all."

"But, sir . . . Sir, very well we have not got a case that could be taken into court. I realise that, sir. But, sir, we ourselves, we know, sir, that those prints were on that whip. And we know also that the same prints were put on to that snap I was taking with me to the fell—to the Sheriff's residence, sir. We know that he killed that girl, sir."

The A.C.P. twitched his moustache. Once. Twice.

"The Sheriff of Bombay is a damned influential person, Ghote," he said. "I am not so sure that I know he murdered that girl, whatever you may be thinking. All right, all right, I accept that they are his prints on that whip. But this girl, she was there for the purposes of prostitution only. She must on many, many occasions have submitted to be whipped when somebody was willing to pay. And if on this occasion the Sheriff, who has I agree a reputation to be an indefatigable Galahad, went too far, well, what the Defence will say is that it was a matter of horseplay only."

Ghote was silent.

Almost he turned away. But then a thought struck him.

"Sir," he said, "it is not a question of one piece of horseplay only. Sir, there have been two murders. Two murders, sir, with the same identical modus operandi. The whipping, sir, followed by the strangling. And, sir, there may have been more such cases before. Cases perhaps not coming under Nagpada P.S. jurisdiction even. Or cases where they have not noted the similar M.O., sir."

"Do you know anything about this second murder, Ghote?" the A.C.P. asked, a look of thoughtfulness settling on his face.

"Only that the victim this time was not a prostitute, sir," Ghote answered. "I am hearing that she was a middle-class girl, a student."

"Yes. Yes, you are right. I have the details here. I am in process of considering whether it is a matter for Crime Branch to show interest in or not."

"Yes, sir."

The A.C.P. dived into one of the wire baskets on his desk. It was labelled *Out*. He scrabbled at the high pile of papers and files in it. Eventually he pulled from it a single sheet and began to read.

"Yes. Yes, just as I thought. The victim was one Miss Veena Bhaskar

—note that name, Ghote, good Brahmin name—known by the name of Sweetie. Student of sociology. Joined for M.A. last year. Aged twenty-two. Father in film distributing line. Very lucrative that, Ghote, as you know. He is a post-graduate also, and the mother is a graduate."

Again the moustache twitched.

Then the A.C.P. looked up.

"I tell you what I am going to do, Inspector," he said. "I am going to take you off all other duties—by the way, what is it you are on now?"

"City Light Cinema chain-snatching case, sir."

"Chain-snatching? For Crime Branch? Ah, yes. Yes, of course. Major-General Whatever-his-name-is. Got anywhere yet?"

"No, sir. No witnesses whatsoever, sir."

"And you've gone through the chain-snatchers file in Records?"

"Yes, sir. Right through it, sir. And there is nothing that makes any of our known subjects particularly likely, sir."

"Hm. Well . . . Well, I tell you what we would do. I will get one of the sub-inspectors to pull in a few of those chain-snatcher fellows and we would see that Major-General Whoever-he-is gets to hear. That should deal with that. And in the meantime you, Ghote, can devote yourself one hundred percent to this damn thing."

"Yes, sir."

Ghote drew himself up to his full height. He knew his eyes were gleaming.

"But, Ghote, understand this. I do not want to be the man in this seat when the Sheriff of Bombay is accused of murder. If I am here, there is to be one hundred percent proof. Two hundred percent proof. Is that understood, Ghote?"

"Yes, sir. Yes, sir, two hundred percent proof."

"And another thing, Ghote."

"Sir?"

"I do not want the Sheriff, if he is innocent only, coming to me and stating that he has been harassed by the police. On no account, Ghote. On no account. You will not interview the fell—You will not interview him. You will not question any of the servants in his house as to his whereabouts at any stated time. You will not tell anyone else you interview that he is in any way involved in our inquiries. Never. In any circumstances. In any circumstances whatsoever."

But at least I can go back to the brothel to see if I can learn anything more about him there, Ghote had thought to himself as staggering almost he had stepped out on to the veranda outside the A.C.P.'s cabin.

Now he stood looking at the place, perhaps half an hour before the evening's business was due to start, a time he calculated when anyone he wished to talk to was bound to be in the house but when there would be little fear of interruption. The "cage" at ground level was as yet without its complement of whores, though as he stood there one of them came in carrying a plastic and a brass bucket and put them side by side in their customary place next to the cupboard-like cubicle at the back where clients and girls could wash. The dirt-sagging curtains which screened off the two cots were still pushed back to reveal the flat mattresses on the beds. On the strip of paint-blistered wooden wall between them there was an oleograph of Mrs. Gandhi garlanded.

The girl straightened from her buckets, gathered up the rattan mat from the uneven concrete floor and, coming to the half-open bars of the room, gave it a none too vigorous shake out into the street. Ghote was reminded abruptly of the whore who had shouted at him on his last visit, "Four rupees on the cot, two only on the mat."

Above, the tall windows from which the more expensive prostitutes from Heera's establishment attracted custom were at the moment devoid of life. The muslin curtains across their top halves moved gently in the occasional puff of late afternoon breeze finding its way into the deep chasm of the street. From one of them a red-and-white striped towel hung limply.

But no doubt inside somewhere the huge *gharwali* was to be found. With any luck she would not as yet have begun her bath and mustard-oil massage that little Munni had spoken of, and she would be free to answer careful questions. Munni, too, might well be worth talking to at greater length. She had said that Kamla was her particular friend and perhaps she would know something about any special clients the dead girl had had in the past. It was pretty well certain, too, that corners-cutting Sub-Inspector D'Silva would not have bothered himself to question her closely about a murder he had plainly not intended to take very seriously.

Oblivious to the busy street life all round him, of the jockeying, hooting rush-hour traffic, of the crudely appetizing smells from the food vendors squatting beside their ramshackle braziers, of the radio music wailing out from the nearest *paan* shop, of the cackle of gossip from the idle pimps and pickpockets, the grandmothers and the street girls, Ghote tried to line up in his mind the questions he could put. At all costs he must not be the first to speak the name of the Sheriff. But he could, surely, ask about clients with more money to spend than the regular visitors to the house, and perhaps then he might acquire evidence about exactly when the Sheriff had been present here and the precise circumstances.

". . . returning for pure pleasure, though pure is not the term I would myself apply to such a disaster area from the hygiene point of view as our good Heera's establishment."

The voice had been loud in his ear, and as soon as he had become aware of it he had recognised the high-pitched, erratic tones. Dr. Framrose, Sexologist, F.R.S.H. (U.K.), his umbrella as ever hanging down his back from his narrow shoulder.

"Doctorji, I am sorry I was not seeing you."

"No, my dear fellow. Your attention was too rigidly fixed on the palace of delights, of dangerous delights, in front of us. But, you know, you are a little early."

"No, no." Ghote felt himself blush. "Please, I assure you, I am not at all here for any such business."

"Oh, you need not pretend with me, my dear chap. I have seen male humanity with, so to speak, its pants down—well, not simply so to speak—in so many disgraceful postures that nothing any longer shocks or surprises me, I promise you."

"Well, yes, I am sure. But—but, well, I am here on duty."

"Oh yes? But not surely in connection with that sad affair last week. A mere prostitute, and an inspector from Crime Branch Headquarters?"

Ghote realised the extent of the quandary he had carelessly placed himself in. He could not reveal to this inquisitive Parsi, a collector of gossip if ever there was one, the real reason for his being here. He could not even stave him off with a few vague hints. The fellow was much too acute for that.

He saw then that there was only one thing for it.

He attempted a carefree laugh, with a hint of bravado about it.

"Well, no," he said. "No, a Headquarterswalla would hardly be here for the murder of such a prostitute only. That fellow D'Silva can take care of that. No, the truth is, Doctor, you have guessed what for I have come."

"Disgraceful fellow," Dr. Framrose said, digging him much harder in the ribs than he liked. "Why can't you chaps stick to your wives? In the dark it makes no difference. No difference at all."

Ghote thought of Protima then, and felt obscurely that he had somehow been unfaithful to her, for all that he had not the least intention of doing in reality what he had told the doctor he would.

At least the fellow was leaving him now. Though not without a parting remark, cackled out in that appallingly loud voice for every chance passer-by to hear.

"And don't forget the one rupee for a condom, my good chap. Money well spent. Money well spent, I can tell you. That thin layer of rubber is almost certainly all that will stand between you and disease. Remember that. Remember that."

Ghote, heedless of everything, plunged forwards for the dark and narrow hallway of the old house.

Climbing cautiously up the steep wooden stairs from which on the last occasion he had been here he had had that sudden, topsy-turvying glimpse of a well-known face, he heard someone coming along the passageway above towards him. A man's tread. The clop of solid *chappals*. For a moment he contemplated turning and hastily leaving. But he was too far up the ladder-like stairs to be able to do so.

The departing visitor came into sight. An astrologer. An old man, his hair a bush of white above the three wide white horizontal lines painted on his forehead. He was clutching his bundle of thick, large-leaved mathematical tables, so untidy that his heavy brown-bead necklace had got caught up in their pages.

Ghote stood sideways on the stairs to let him pass, receiving as he did so a mingled whiff of stale body odour and unctuous jasmine.

No doubt the fellow had been visiting Heera. Had he told her that she would soon be meeting a hostile stranger? A man in an official position? And that she should take care not to reveal any secrets?

More to the point, would she, having been delayed perhaps by the consultation, be hurrying now to have that bath and oil massage from Munni?

He took the remaining stairs at a fast climb, hardly paused at the passage with its three flimsy doors where the poor Svashbuckler had been so sick, and made for the next flight up.

As, loudly and stampingly, he arrived at the floor above, a girl, or rather woman, took a pace out of one of the three doors in the passage at this level. By her sari, thickly embellished with tinselly *jari*-work, he saw that she was one of Heera's whores, a tallish creature, showing every sign of a beautiful body under the gaudy sari, with a face long, unsmiling and faintly pock-marked.

No sooner had she seen him than she stepped quickly back. Ghote heard muttering female voices.

He guessed that they must be coming from Heera's own room, and before she could give an order to close its door he strode rapidly along the passage and boldly entered, fixing a look of simple friendliness on his face.

"It is Heerabai?" he asked. "I was seeing you a few nights ago, the night poor Kamla died."

The huge *gharwali* was lying on a wide, wooden bed, its elaborately carved head set with small enamel plaques depicting bunches of red roses. She was dressed today in a dark green sari, as deeply gold-edged as had been the thigh-stretched red one.

"I am not liking policewallas," she said, raising herself up a little on one massive forearm decorated with a tattoo of curling leaves.

Ghote tried a careless smile and deliberately dropped into an easy stance, leaning against the edge of the open doorway. He would have liked to have flopped down on to the foot of the wide bed occupying most of the room, but he thought that this might be too provocative.

"I am sure you are liking my friend Sub-Inspector D'Silva," he said. "And I am sure he is very much liking some of your girls."

But the sprawling creature on the bed showed no signs of relenting.

"He is wanting his *hafta,*" she said. "He is getting. What else can a poor woman do but pay and pay?"

"Well, at least I am not wanting rupees," Ghote answered. "And not a short-time with any of your girls either."

A quick frown appeared on Heera's broad forehead under the dangling glass jewel she wore there.

"Then what are you wanting?" she asked. "What are you wanting, Inspector Sahib?"

Inwardly Ghote winced. He was not going to learn anything if this creature continued to be so hostile, and none of the approaches he had tried so far had gone any way towards softening her. There seemed to be nothing for it but to come out more or less directly with the subject he had in mind.

He sighed.

"Oh," he said, "I am just a little interested only in a fellow I saw here the last time I came. That was with Dr. Framrose, you remember, and an Englishman, a film star, a very very famous English film star."

Would such oblique flattery work the trick for him?

"Film star, dim star," fat Heera answered. "He is not Amitabh is he? Not Sashi Kapoor?"

"Well, in England," Ghote lied, "he is as well known. A very very great star."

"England is far away."

Heera lapsed into silence, stonily massive silence.

"Well," Ghote said again after a little, "do you know what person it was I was meaning?"

"What meaning?"

At least she was talking.

"Who I was meaning when I asked about the man I saw here that night, the *bahadur,* the rich man."

"I am not knowing any such people."

The statement was as flat and uncompromising as anything she had said yet. Here was a wall he was not going to be able to surmount. Unless he could do it by pretending to know more than he was certain of.

He pushed himself up from the door jamb, strolled with deliberate insolence over to the bed and plunked himself down.

"Come," he said, "no need for all this bluff between you and me. I know who he was, and so do you. Just tell me what you know about him."

Heera looked at him. Her eyebrows, thick and unplucked, were drawn together in a straight line above her half-closed eyes. There was a sticky silence in the little room. In its far corner, next to the carved bedhead, the whore Heera had sent to see who had been coming stood as still as if she were another carved object.

"Him?" Heera said at last. "What him only? I am not knowing any him. What for are you asking and asking these questions?"

Ghote, cursing inwardly, shrugged as casually as he could.

"Oh, he was a fellow I thought I recognised," he said. "But perhaps I was wrong. I was coming along Falkland Road just now and I thought I would drop in and ask. Just to see if my guess had been right."

"Well, it was not. Now, go. Unless you are wanting to pay for a girl?"

"No. No, no."

He got up. He was, he had to admit, beaten. There was no way he could get information out of this fat sprawl of a woman. Not if she was unwilling to give it while he was prevented from saying a certain name and then using brutal tactics to extract from her what she knew. Yet he was not going to leave tamely admitting this defeat.

He looked hard at the creature on the bed.

"Well, I am going now," he said. "But I would be seeing you again. Many times perhaps."

He stepped into the doorway, and then, over his shoulder, added a careless-seeming request.

"That little girl of yours, the one who found Kamla, is she anywhere about?"

He had been watching Heera covertly as he had put his question and he distinctly caught the gleam of malice that came into her eyes.

"It is Munni you are meaning. Well, she has gone. Been sold. Days ago. And I am not at all knowing where she is now. Not at all."

This was a blow. As increasingly the *gharwali* had shown she had no intention of revealing anything at all, he had turned his mind more and more to little, bright Munni. Here was someone who earlier had shown no disinclination to talk. She had, of course, told him she did not know who had been with Kamla just before she had found her. But at that time he had not had an opportunity, or indeed any duty, to ask her more. To inquire, for instance, about any rich clients Kamla had ever had who had enjoyed whipping her.

But now, just as he had decided with some pleasure that he would circumvent Heera's obstinacy by seeing the plump and joyous little girl, he had been told that she had been sold. Nor would it do him any good, plainly, to ask which other brothel she had been sold to. Heera

had already indicated that she might have been passed on to yet somewhere else. It was the common custom in Kamatipura for girls to be
moved from place to place as the ebb and flow of business dictated.
And the *gharwali* had clearly been determined, he saw now, to take
advantage of this to keep him or anybody else, from finding out about
a client of hers who valued discretion and was no doubt prepared to
pay heavily for it.

In other circumstances he could have hauled the fat madam into
Headquarters and questioned her till she dropped. But that would
only draw attention to the person he wanted to get at, and any such
move had been banned by the A.C.P. in terms that defied looking for
loopholes.

But he must get hold of Munni, all the more so since it now looked
as if she might have some information which Heera wished to keep
secret.

Thumping disconsolately down the steep stairs, he realised that
only one course lay open to him. He would have to go to Sub-Inspector D'Silva, that most knowledgeable of persons about the ins-and-outs
of Kamatipura, and, doing his best to assume the happy back-slapping
tone the fellow habitually used, he would have to pick his brains.

And at the same time tell him nothing. It was a daunting prospect.

He emerged from the house and stood for a moment on the black,
uneven stones of the pavement facing the cacophony of the street.
The traffic was beginning to thin out and it would soon be dark but
the noise was hardly less. Already the first customers were beginning
to come along the length of the road, looking into the Cages where the
lights—glaring blue neon or warmer orangey tones—were here and
there flickering into life. From above, a few of the better-class prostitutes were shouting down to men who looked as if they could be
persuaded to come up, and yelling obscenities at them if they passed
on.

"Sahib! Sahib! Sahib!"

Was that a girl calling to him? From right above where he was
standing? Such impudence.

He turned and stepped over the stinking drain trickling with foul
black liquid and into the roadway where it was easier to walk. A wildly
frantic hissing followed him.

So frantic that he actually, without thinking, looked back to see who was making it.

With a jolt of surprise he found it was the whore who had been standing like a carved wooden statue in Heera's room. And she was signalling him now. Signalling plainly not an invitation to go on to one of the beds with her but an invitation to meet inside the brightly lit, not far distant Olympia Café.

8

Ghote walked slowly along the roadway towards the Olympia Café through the as yet thin drifting streams of would-be brothel customers, stepping up on to the pavement from time to time when forced to by a taxi or a horse-drawn victoria threading its way along.

What could that girl or woman—she must be in her late twenties from the look he had got of her—what could she want with him? There could be no mistaking that she had urgently indicated that she wanted to meet him. But why? Could it possibly be to give him the information that she had listened to fat Heera so obstinately withholding? But would every whore in the house know the Sheriff's identity? Surely not. Certainly none of them was very likely to have recognised him. Brothel girls seldom left the houses they were in, let alone the Kamatipura area. There was too much danger of them absconding for that, either on their own because they hated the life or with some lover, a pickpocket or other hanger-on from nearby.

Well, nothing else to do but wait and see. If the girl came. If she could even get out of Heera's house to come.

Deep in thought he nearly knocked into a *dhupwalla* going from brothel to brothel with his smoking brass pot of purifying incense at the start of the evening's activities. The sweet reek of its greyish smoke briefly stung his nostrils.

There were a few vacant tables in the big, mirror-walled café with, as he entered, its jukebox belting out a Muslim religious *quwali* and its waiters going round setting out glasses of water or using their sodden mopping-up rags. Ghote chose a small table as much out of the way as possible but with a clear sight of the big doors.

Would the girl come?

One of the waiters approached and he ordered two Thums Up, one for his surprise guest. If she kept her rendezvous. He had just received the bottles of dark red, gently fizzing drink clouded with condensation from the refrigerated cabinet when he saw her.

Yes, she was a fine woman, her breasts ample without being too much so, her stomach flat as a chapatti, her bearing proud. Only her face echoed none of the voluptuousness of her body. It was, even from the hasty glance from side to side she gave as soon as she had crossed the threshold, sullenly set.

She hurried across and sat swiftly on the other bentwood chair at the narrow, marble-topped, crack-seamed table.

"I ordered for a Thums Up," Ghote said. "I hope it is what you like?"

"Yes, yes."

She brushed aside the query and leant eagerly towards him.

"I must not stay long," she said. "Heerabai would beat me if she finds I have left the house."

So, surely, she did intend to defy the *gharwali* and tell him something that was meant to be kept secret.

"Yes," he said. "Then tell me what you want to. I am listening. What is your name?"

She pursed her lips momentarily as if making up her mind exactly how to say whatever it was that she had taken such a risk to come and tell him.

Then she spoke.

"I am Putla by name," she said. "And I am not knowing just why you were asking those questions in the house. I had thought S.I. D'Silva was the in-charge for Kamla's death. But whatever your reason I am going to tell you what Heerabai would not."

That it had been the Sheriff with Kamla that night? That the Sheriff had been the only person to use that room before the girl's death?

Was he going to have that much luck at the very start?

"Yes," he said. "Speak, speak."

"It is difficult for Heerabai," Putla answered, keeping her voice low and leaning even closer. "You know what her life has been?"

"No. No."

What does it matter, her life, he had wanted to say. But he saw that he had to be as careful as possible with this creature. Otherwise she could be on her feet, out of the café and back under Heera's wing in no time.

"Heera was a devadasi," Putla said. "She is from Belgaum District where there were many devadasis in the temples for men to come to when she was a girl. Many times she has told us how when she was a little, little girl only she was becoming very ill. Her father was not at home. He had had to go some distance for work. So her grandmother and her mother dedicated her to Goddess Yellamma if she got well. In time that illness passed, so when she was old enough her grandmother and mother wished to take her to the temple to become a devadasi. But her father did not at all want that for her. He wanted for her to be decently married and not be having to take every man that came. But all the village cried out against him because if he did what he wanted for Heera it would anger Goddess Yellamma. For many days he resisted and resisted. But at last all the voices in the village were too strong for him, and he left his house one day and was never seen again."

Putla fell silent. It was plain that she was seeing in her mind's eye that lonely departure.

Ghote wondered why she was telling him the story. It was sad, of course. Still, things like that no longer happened since the passing of the Devadasi Act. Or did they?

But was he ever going to hear the identity of the man who had been with Kamla just before she had been killed?

"Go on," he said. "You should not take too much of time."

Putla gave an anxious glance at the café doors.

"There is not much more," she said. "Soon a man was found for Heera to co-habit with as a devadasi. For some time she did that, but before long the man was no more interested. So then there was no one to support Heera, and she ran away to Bombay to be with other prostitutes. She was like us once, with no money and with debts even. But at last she was able to save little by little and also, I think, she had a rich man who gave to her, or was made to give. And at last she could rent first one room for two girls and then more until she had as many as she has now."

"Yes, yes. But why are you telling this?"

"It is because Heerabai is a mother to me, to show why she was keeping silent in the house just now and to make you see she will never betray any rich man."

Any rich man? Would it come now? The name. Or even a good description?

"With me it was different," Putla said abruptly after a short silence.

Ghote swore inwardly. If she went on as she had been, she might suddenly feel that she had risked spending too much time outside the house, get up and rush away with nothing said to his purpose. But to try to force her off the path she seemed to have chosen might be to cut off the flow more decisively.

"Yes?" he said, looking at her with as much of a show of interest as he could rise to.

"I am educated," she said. "I am matriculate, you know. And in my native-place I had employment, working for a doctor. He was of a different community, but he liked me and I liked him. Then one day after he had finished his work he made love to me. After some time we became lovers and I could think of nothing but him only. Until after one year I heard one day he had got married, to a girl in his own community. Then, in that moment, I became cold. And what could I do when I could no longer work for that man and I had no face to go back again to my parents' place?"

Once more she fell silent. And once more inwardly Ghote cursed.

"Go on," he said. "I am listening to your story."

"So I decided to come to Bombay also," Putla resumed. "To make money from these hypocrites and these characterless skunks. Sometimes I am not even opening my legs and yet they must pay."

She glared at Ghote violently as if he were a characterless skunk himself.

Damn her. Why would she not tell him what it was she had come here to tell?

"Listen," he said. "You want to give me the answers that Heera would not. But you must not stay here long. So tell me. Tell me now."

"Yes, I will tell. I will tell and tell. Because of what that bastard did to Kamla."

"That bastard? Then you know his name?"

A moment of wild hope.

"No, no. How could I be knowing that? He is one of the rich ones who come early and enter by the back way. They go to whoever they are always liking, and we others never see them."

"One of the rich ones?" Ghote asked, his optimism fading fast. "There are many?"

"No, no. Two-three perhaps four. Do you think many rich men would come to a brothel like Heera's only? They would go to Sukhlaji Street, if they are coming to this part at all."

"But do you know anything about him? This man who killed Kamla?"

"No. Nothing. Nothing at all."

"Then why? Why have you come out here when Heera would beat you if she is finding out?"

"Because I can tell you one thing. I can tell you where is little Munni, and she was very, very much friends with Kamla. Perhaps she would give you that man's name. Or tell all about him, you know."

"Yes. Good. Where? Where is she?"

"She has been sent to Saroja's house, not sold but sent. That much I was hearing."

"Saroja's house? Where is that?"

"I do not know. It is in Kamatipura somewhere, but I am not knowing just where. But Saroja is a friend of Heerabai's, and she has been given Munni until the danger is past."

"But Saroja's, have you any idea where it is?"

"No. No. I must go now. Heerabai will be wanting to give us the blessing before the first customer comes. I must go."

She jumped up from the table.

"No. Wait. Stay."

But she had not in the least heeded his low, urgent pleas. And in a moment he realised that it would be sheer idiocy to make a scene in a place like the Olympia. Every second customer was a street prostitute or a pimp or a pickpocket and they would be only too delighted to gossip about an incident of this sort and perhaps even to make sure news of it got back to Heera.

He rose slowly from his chair and went to pay for the two Thums Up.

He would still, he thought, have to go to Sub-Inspector D'Silva. If anyone could tell him quickly where any particular *gharwali* had her establishment it would be D'Silva. But asking him about this Saroja, and making himself so agreeable that he got a straight and quick answer, was not going to be something he would like doing. Not in the least.

At the Nagpada Police Station Ghote found to his added dismay that D'Silva was not on duty. Nor could anyone else he saw tell him which of the scores of brothels in the area was "Saroja's house."

"D'Silva would know, Inspector," an assistant sub-inspector said. "Trust him. But he is out on the town somewhere. You know that boy. Somewhere different to put his middle leg every night."

He winked and, had Ghote not stepped sharply back, would have poked him in the ribs.

"Do you know where tonight D'Silva could be found?" he asked coldly. "It is most urgent that I see him."

The A.S.I. put on a heavy-thinking face.

"Aunty joint?" he said. "He likes a drink also, and in a place like an aunty joint he would get all he wants for free. You should try Wine Cottage out at Worli. That is somewhere he is very much liking. But then he may be at a Mujra Nite. That he is liking also, or the girls that are working there. They are free for him, isn't it? But, yes, now I am thinking. He said he would be at Plaza Restaurant in Colaba Causeway. He has a piece of business later for a friend in Vigilante Branch, Colaba P.S. Yes, yes. You would find him at that place just now."

With growing grim determination Ghote made his way south to the colourful, cosmopolitan tip of sea-surrounded Bombay where the tourists and the Western hippies mingled with the beggars and the shopkeepers and the people who chose to live there because it represented the free-and-easy city at its most careless. He had passed on many occasions the big Plaza Restaurant with its huge sign advertising *Daily Captivating Cabarets* and *Sexciting Performances,* the shows that were labelled *Mujra Nites* in distant imitation of the famed dances of elegant, once-upon-a-time Lucknow where to the skilled playing of court musicians girls of renowned beauty performed on floors of marble scattered with rose petals.

He had never been into the place, however, and he approached it now with a certain amount of caution. Best, he decided, to proclaim himself straight away as police and ask if D'Silva was there, rather than pretend to be just an ordinary customer and go looking for him himself.

At once when he announced his identity to the manager, a young man boldly dressed in European tuxedo and bright red bow-tie, he was made effusively welcome.

"But you must talk Hindi only please," the fellow said. "I am B.A. failed but matric pass. You are always most welcome here, Inspectorji. You must come many, many more times. We are having such a great success always."

He cast his eyes up to the plaster ceiling of the entrance foyer.

"Success we are owing to the One above," he went cascadingly on, his Hindi mingled with odd English expressions. "Sixteen girls we are showing every night. Well, it is really seven-eight only, but they are all the time changing their costumes and their names also. So it is the same thing. Yes?"

"Yes, if you like," Ghote answered. "But where is Sub-Inspector D'Silva? I am wanting to see him most urgently."

"Of course, of course, Inspectorji. You policewallas, always urgent-urgent business. A little *hafta* here, a little there, isn't it?"

He rubbed the palm of his hand in the traditional money-getting gesture.

"D'Silva," Ghote said sharply. "Where can I find?"

"I will show. I will show. This way only, Inspectorji, and you will be able to see our *world-famed* dancers also. Sub-Inspectorji is watching, or he is *backstage* only, talk-talking. And other things, yes?"

Ghote remained silent. At least he was being led to the restaurant auditorium. There with any luck he would spot D'Silva for himself. Once more he cursed first the girl Putla for not knowing where the house was where he could get hold of little Munni, and perhaps then learn for certain that the Sheriff had been with Kamla, and next D'Silva for forcing him to come to such an appalling place as this, so far beneath the dignity of a police officer.

Then, passing through a pair of swinging doors, he was in a moment overwhelmed by a blare of noise and confusion of light. The restaurant itself was darkened but from its ceiling a mirror-studded revolving globe caught in a spotlight of ever-changing colours threw blobs and splashes of red, blue and green over the assembled, seemingly all male, audience. Only the platform at the far end, where a band dressed for some reason as South American gauchos was belting out music, was blazingly lit.

Dammit, he thought, I will never see D'Silva in all this.

"D'Silva?" he hissed furiously into the manager's ear. "Where is he? Now?"

"But, look. Look, Inspectorji," the fellow replied, not keeping his voice down at all. "Look on the stage. There is the beautiful Suraiya dancing." His voice did drop a little then. "And soon she will be the beautiful Mehmooda," he added.

Ghote cast an eye at the bright rectangle of the platform.

The girl dancing there, her face powdered a dead white, a gash of red at her lips, was fat. But her dance, or rather act, was being greeted with enthusiasm. It made great play with a cigarette and each blatant obscenity was greeted with whistles and shouts—from members of the band in chorus if they were not spontaneously forthcoming from the audience.

Ghote found no difficulty in looking away.

"Where is D'Silva?" he demanded once again.

"Must be *backstage*," the manager answered, evidently resigning himself to not capturing another police officer. "We will go. You will see the girls in the flesh only, Inspectorji. And such flesh. You may please touch also."

Ghote did not think it likely that he would feel any desire to do that. Grimly he followed the manager round the side of the darkened, colour-splotched restaurant until at last they reached an unobtrusive door beside the stage.

On the far side the scene was very different. All the tinsel glamour was, as it were, ripped away. Instead there was squalor unadorned. The walls everywhere seen in the harsh light of a few neon tubes were smeared with greasy black and stained splotchily with rusty red expectorated *paan* juice. Pervasively there was the smell of dried urine.

But at least the manager was asking people where D'Silva was to be found. And getting answers.

In a few moments he pushed open a door decorated with a glittering silver star—peeling away at one side—and there in what was evidently, despite its distinguishing sign, a mere communal dressing room was D'Silva.

He was standing with his hand on the bare shoulder of a young girl in process of transforming herself from a Bharat Natyam dancer in an appallingly crude red muslin sari into a Muslim beauty in a Moghul outfit in equally crude black and gold. She was leaning slightly forward, apparently oblivious of D'Silva's hand, peering into a mirror surrounded by a few light bulbs and applying green make-up to her eyelids.

"Well, well, it is Ghote," D'Silva said. "I seem always to be finding you among naughty girls. Didn't think you had it in you, Ganesh *bhai.*"

He brought his hand sliding down the half-transformed girl's back as she leant at the mirror and gave her a cheerful slap.

"How would you like this little darling?" he asked. "She's a jumping cracker in bed, I tell you."

"I am afraid I am here on duty only, D'Silva," Ghote answered. "There is a piece of information you can give me, just something I need to know. A *gharwali* called Saroja. Can you tell me where exactly in Kamatipura her house is?"

"Ah, Saroja. Yes. Ha, you have picked yourself a good one there, Ganesh *bhai.* But you will not get what you're looking for there for nothing. Not unless I take you myself and say you're a friend. Pays very high *hafta,* Saroja. And for that she can keep out whoever she wants. Except me."

"I do not want . . ." Ghote began.

But then he thought: he might not want what Saroja had to offer without payment, but he did want to get into her good graces. If he was to talk to plump little Munni quietly on her own and learn all she had to tell about Kamla's special client, then he would certainly be much better off with D'Silva's introduction.

"Well, yes, on second thoughts," he said. "Perhaps you would as a favour take me there and tell Saroja I am your friend."

D'Silva shook a finger in mock reproof.

"And all the time at Headquarters," he said, "I was thinking you were a goody-goody fellow, Inspector, just like old D'Sa. Never a thought of going elsewhere but to the wife."

Ghote decided that all he could do was to ignore such remarks.

"Could we go to Saroja's now?" he asked. "It would be very, very helpful to me."

"Can't do, man," D'Silva said.

"But, please. Of course, I am seeing that you are having a nice time here, but, believe me, I am very much wishing to meet this Saroja."

"You should take a cold shower, man," D'Silva answered. "Calm yourself down. Don't want to spoil things by being overexcited, you know."

"No, it is not—"

"No. But trouble is, man, I've made a promise to a friend, an assistant inspector at Colaba P.S. He's looking for a dummy client to raid a posh brothel, and I promised I would do it. I'm just the boy for it, an' all."

"But when is this?" Ghote asked, seeing any chance of getting to Munni that night vanishing away.

"Oh, in half an hour or so," D'Silva replied. "Hey, tell you what. You come too. Lend a touch of realism. The reluctant client tagging along also. I like it. Then afterwards I'll take you to Saroja, and you can release any hot feelings you have not been able to satisfy where we're going. What you say, Inspector?"

"All right," Ghote said.

Ghote was never quite sure where exactly the flat that they raided was, only that it was somewhere in the Nariman Point area among all the brutishly new towering blocks of offices and luxury apartments built on land not long reclaimed from the sea. Driving fast through the darkness in D'Silva's car he caught a glimpse of the signboard outside one block he knew, Jolly Maker Chambers, but almost immediately afterwards his sense of direction deserted him.

But soon D'Silva had brought the car to a halt, a tyre-screaming one, and they were padding up a carpeted staircase in the semidark.

A carpeted staircase, Ghote had just time to think. A very posh place. Lots and lots of money flowing.

Then D'Silva knocked in a particular rhythm on a door bearing the name-plate *P. D. Unwalla* and after a few tense moments of waiting they were let in.

The place looked as rich in decoration inside as the carpeted stairs leading up to it had foreshadowed. The walls of its hallway were papered in an opulent shade of green and hung with colourful masks made by tribals. The light came from a sharply glittering chandelier.

P. D. Unwalla himself, gently plump, double-chinned and soft-eyed, hailed D'Silva as an old acquaintance—though he did greet him as "Mr. Fonseca"—and gestured towards a long padded bench that ran the length of the hallway.

"Sit, sit," he invited.

D'Silva kicked off his shoes and planked himself down expectantly on the squishy bench. Ghote, slower, followed suit.

Almost at once through a door at the far end of the hall there emerged four girls, all good-looking in very much the same healthy way, each dressed in a daringly thin, body-showing Kota sari. They descended on the bench like so many fluttering-winged pigeons.

It did not take D'Silva more than a couple of minutes to make up his mind. But there was a further period of discussion before P. D. Unwalla, with a sigh at his own kindness, agreed on a price of a hundred and fifty rupees. The money, large, scuffed and dirty notes, changed hands.

"And you, my friend," P. D. Unwalla said to Ghote as D'Silva disappeared with his chosen girl behind the first door leading off the hallway. "You are slow to choose."

"I—I am not feeling so well," Ghote said, and indeed his voice was sounding convincingly croaky. "Perhaps I will wait for some time."

"By all means, by all means. But do not linger too long. Others may come, and you will lose your choice."

"Yes, yes. I would not be too long."

Ghote attempted a smile.

When the hell would the police party D'Silva had spoken of arrive?

But he did not in the end have to sit for very long making conversation—in a fashion he knew to be desperately feeble—to the three remaining Kota sari-clad girls. After what he guessed was exactly ten minutes from the time of their own arrival there came another knock on the front door, in the same characteristic rhythm.

P. D. Unwalla reappeared, drew back the bolt on the door and opened it confidently.

"Police," barked a voice from outside and a booted foot was thrust in.

An assistant inspector in uniform pushed his way inside then, followed by two constables looking very pleased with themselves and gawping at the flat's luxuries with evident pleasure. Looking much less pleased, indeed distinctly apprehensive, there came next the two *panches,* necessary witnesses according to the law to any police raid or arrest.

The assistant inspector went straight to the door behind which

D'Silva had vanished, and jerked it open. A moment or two later D'Silva appeared.

"I require your name under the provisions of the Suppression of Immoral Traffic Act 1958," the assistant inspector said to him with straight-faced formality. "And I call upon you to note that I have found you in a compromising position with a person of the female sex."

D'Silva, play-acting the caught client for all he was worth, zipping his trouser fly and grinning with pantomime sheepishness, supplied the information mandatory under the act, always known as SITA 1958.

P. D. Unwalla was then searched and the notes D'Silva had handed to him were shown with swift ceremoniousness to the two overawed *panches*.

Ghote thought then that the affair was concluded, and his mind turned again to Kamatipura and Saroja's house, wherever that might be.

But he was in for a surprise. The constables escorted out the bewildered *panches*. Then as soon as the door had closed behind them D'Silva revealed himself with a grin to P. D. Unwalla as a police officer. There followed some hurried muttered conversation which Ghote was unable to hear.

He saw quite clearly, however, the next stage in the proceedings. It was the passing over of a very much larger number of high denomination notes than the sum D'Silva, or "Mr. Fonseca," had given to P. D. Unwalla on his first arrival. There followed relieved and friendly smiles from police and potentially prosecuted equally.

"Right, Inspector," D'Silva said at last, turning to Ghote. "Let's go, man."

Ghote felt a surge of fury. He had neatly been made an accomplice to an act of bribery, a transaction he would never in the ordinary way have countenanced for all that he knew such things were a regular occurrence. But he had no way of venting that anger. Much less could he report the matter to the Anti-Corruption Bureau. Not if he wanted to get as quickly as possible to meet again little, knowledgeable Munni.

For that he depended on D'Silva. And if he wanted to make use of him he must turn an entirely blind eye to this piece of flagrant law-breaking.

"Very well, S.I.," he said. "Let's go."

9

Saroja's house proved to be a bungalow of two storeys in Sukhlaji
Street, one of the better places in a district where the brothels ranged
from something hardly above the squalor of the hutment slums of the
city to old houses achieving a fair standard of order and cleanliness.
Ghote was delighted to see the place at last. During all his journey
with D'Silva from Nariman Point up to Kamatipura through the now
quietening night streets he had been regaled with the sub-inspector's
views on life.

"Man, when you find a fool like that Unwalla you got to milk him
for all he's worth, and did we do it tonight."

Ghote's contribution to that had been simply stubborn silence.

"Murder? You can't call a girl like that five-rupeewali getting killed
the other night murder. It's not worth doing more than filling in a
First Information Report."

"So you have not found a likely offender, S.I.?"

A bark of a laugh.

"And don't intend to, man. Where would I look? Might have been
anyone in the whole of Bombay, all bloody seven million of them. No,
if murder's going to interest me, it'd have to be one of the really
greats."

"A great murderer?"

"You bet, Ganesh *bhai*. No reason why a murderer shouldn't be
great. Take that Jack the Ripper in England, in the past sometime. His
name's gone down in history, isn't it? Now, if I'd solved that case I'd
have got my name in the history books, too. Francis D'Silva. That's the
sort of affair I'd really get down to cracking, man."

Ghote had read about Jack the Ripper once, somewhere. The details were vague in his mind, but he thought the fellow had killed five
or six prostitutes in London and there had been a great *hungama* about

it with all sorts of people being named later as the killer. Even some British prince.

And the man who had killed miserable Kamla and now a second girl in the same manner, and perhaps already others where the modus operandi had not been remarked on, was he not very much the same as that British fellow? And was he not also—it was very, very likely— the Sheriff of Bombay?

But D'Silva—*Aiee,* so his name is Francis not Charlie—had made a hero out of the Englishman. Really, he was altogether too much of a boasting type.

"Hey, you've read the Kama Sutra at least?"

D'Silva's loud inquiry had broken in on his dark thoughts.

"Yes," he lied quickly. "Everyone has done that."

Well, he had seen copies of it. Tattered, finger-marked copies in the hands of schooldays friends.

And in the Sheriff's richly furnished private room, behind the glass of his bookcase, that eight-hundred-rupee edition.

"Okay, I'll tell you something it says all the same. If you ever did read it, I bet you skimmed the pages with your eyes all the time looking round for some grown-up."

Again Ghote's reply had been silence.

"Okay. There's this bit in it about the messenger of love. You know, the fellow who fixes up a girl for a rich man. Well, listen to what qualities that chap has to have, according to old Vatsyayana. I by-hearted the list. Let me see. There's eloquence, courage, insight, cool-headedness, reliability, deception, resourcefulness and finally quick action. You know what other kind of person needs all those?"

Evidently an answer expected.

"No."

"I'll tell you, man. The detective. Isn't it? Talking your way into places, not being damn scared, seeing beyond the fronts they put up, keeping your cool, doing what you say you will, cheating the buggers if they need it—oh, and being, as they put it on your Service Sheet, resourceful. Plus quick-acting. Am I right, man? Am I right?"

"Yes."

But at last they had reached Sukhlaji Street.

And now to get himself into the good graces of the madam of the house in front of them he had to rely on the fellow who had gloried in comparing a pimp to a police officer.

Ghote gave the place a sharp assessing glance as D'Silva piloted him towards it. At its door there lounged a man whose appearance in every particular, from oiled hair blatantly imitating that of No. 1 superstar Amitabh to extra-narrow pants turned up at the bottoms and held in place by a jazzy belt, announced him as a *goonda*.

So . . . the house ran to a private bully-boy guard. And, yes, there in the lamplight was a glimpse of the hilt of a *rampuri* knife at his waist. The vicious leather-scraper's tool, a favourite weapon with the worst of the *goondas*.

Above the house door, again catching the feeble light from the nearest lamp, was the street number, a great deal more boldly displayed than those of most Bombay establishments. A sign specially for the naïve that this was somehow a licensed place, safer and cleaner than the brothels of Falkland Road or the yet lower places in the Kamatipura lanes.

D'Silva gave a cool nod to the *goonda* and walked straight in. Ghote followed.

Would Munni really be here? And if she was, and if he could contrive to see her on her own, would she be able to tell him enough? Enough to confirm, or possibly even to upset, his belief that it was the Sheriff of Bombay who had killed her friend Kamla? Who had killed once more already. And would, unless he was stopped, kill and kill and kill again.

At the top of a short flight of neatly rubber-treaded stairs, wider and far cleaner than those at the Falkland Road place, they entered a small hall, a big bright room, its floor colourfully tiled, a cheerful pattern of red tiles and white running halfway up its walls. From the ornate ceiling there hung a large brass lantern with coloured glass sides as well as two easily swirling fans, their blades notable where dust and grime so often accumulated for their cleanliness. At the far end above the entrance to a second flight of stairs there was a clock, golden-framed, an object that said much about the type of client the place attracted, men in whose lives time counted.

But most of this Ghote registered only in retrospect. There were benches round the walls covered in bright red leather and on them were sitting the brothel's girls, many in short Western skirts and low-cut blouses, together with a handful of waiting customers. Rapidly he looked along the rows of them for the plump and pretty form of little Munni.

Not there.

But that might well mean she was with a customer. Down the stairs on the far side just as they had come in one of the girls had come leading by the hand a portly grinning businessman and at once a girl from the benches had led off her own particular catch. Munni, if she were here at all, must be in one of the rooms up the stairs. And she would probably not be there very long.

A woman of about fifty, hard-faced and almost soldier-like in bearing under her black sari with a plentiful edging of gold, came towards them.

"Saroja," D'Silva greeted her. "I have brought you a new customer, fellow raring to go."

He dropped his voice a little.

"One of us," he said. "Inspector, too. So be good to him."

Ghote found himself subjected to an unyielding stare that made him wish for a moment that he was wearing a better shirt, looking more of a spender.

Saroja, he thought, would not be an easy one to bluff. He would be likely to need all the deception and resourcefulness of that go-between in the Kama Sutra if he was to get to Munni without her suspecting anything.

"D'Silva Sahib," Saroja said, turning away at last, "what can I do for you tonight? I have someone fresh-fresh. A little Punjabi, only sixteen. Lovely."

D'Silva grinned.

"For me just now, nothing," he said. "I have some business to finish. But I'll be back, my dear. If not tonight, maybe tomorrow, eh?"

He gave the madam a savage wink, turned on his heel and left.

"Now for you, Inspector?" Saroja inquired. "We have every sort of girl. You have only to say what is your taste. And you can stay however long you want, short-time, double-time, double-extra and tea in the morning. Whatever you like."

In an almost instant decision Ghote made up his mind to play along. Better by far to let this tough-looking creature believe he had come only to go with one of her girls than to indicate to her in any way that he was interested in the one from Falkland Road she had been entrusted with.

"Thank you very much," he said. "I will look and choose. You have some A1 nice-looking girls."

"As you like, Inspector. As you like."

Saroja left and Ghote strolled slowly up and down the room, half pretending to look at the whores, half spying out the land.

Suddenly there came a loud question from one of the girls, evidently demanded of the man waiting with her, a bushy-bearded jovial Sikh.

"Respect and honour?" she shouted. "Where to find respect and honour?"

The Sikh, sitting with his arm round the girl, at once put on an expression of profound thought. But he did not offer any answer.

Nor, Ghote thought, had he any answer himself to the ridiculous query. A prostitute concerned about respect? A girl as worn as a temple stair, as they said? Really.

But from across the other side of the hall an answer came. A girl there bounced to her feet, cupped her generous breasts with her two hands and offered them to the assembly.

"Respect and honour," she shouted back. "You find them here."

"No, no," called another girl, kicking her plump legs high. "They are here. Here."

"No, here," came a third response as yet another whore jumped up, turned round, bent over the red bench and favoured the company with a vigorous wiggle of her skirted behind.

But the diversion did not last long. Girls with customers came down the stairs back into the room. Girls led off their prizes up the stairs.

And no sign of Munni.

Then Ghote saw that the girl he had first seen taking a customer off was returning with him. And soon the next one to go had come back.

He realised that he could go on pretending to be making his choice no longer. Perhaps Munni was being kept hidden here to the extent of not being allowed to appear in the hall for customers to choose. He would have to launch into more positive action, even if it meant taking a risk.

And Saroja was approaching him, swaying seductively in that clinging black sari for all her years.

"Still you have not chosen anyone?" she said.

He caught a whiff of almond oil from her skin. Thick and cloying. "No," he replied.

Then he took a quick apprehensive breath.

"Well, to tell you the truth," he ventured, "I believe you have a new girl here that I am hearing about. Nice and young, and very much smiling always. And a little plump. I was hoping for her."

Saroja looked back at him in silence, her face stonily hard.

He licked his lips.

"I think I am hearing her name even," he said. "It was—it was beginning with M."

He paused. Saroja remained silent.

"Mala, was it?" he said. "Or Manju? Or—or Munni. Yes. Yes, I am thinking it was Munni."

And with that a look of bleak triumph flooded on to Saroja's face, and flicked away again as quickly.

At once Ghote realised two things. The first, oddly, was that, despite her name, Saroja was not a woman. She was a *hijra,* one of the female-leaning men that someone like Dr. Framrose, sex changes, would have operated on, if such an operation had been undertaken with any medical supervision. D'Silva must have deliberately kept him in the dark over the madam's true nature in the hope he would make a fool of himself. Getting an innocent to go with a eunuch was, after all, a standard joke in this part of Bombay.

But what was more serious was the realisation that his gamble had not come off. It had been a bad mistake not somehow to have contrived—though it was hard to see how—never to have mentioned Munni's name. Because it was clear beyond doubt now that she was indeed here in the house and hidden. Hidden from himself.

The eunuch's swift look of self-justifying triumph had confirmed that for him plainly as if it had been written down in his notebook.

"Have you got such a girl as that Munni here?" he asked nevertheless, still retaining what artlessness he could.

"No," said Saroja. "No. You must take someone else, Inspector."

The eunuch gave him a stony stare in which he detected the tiniest hint of malice.

"No, I have no Munni here," he went on. "So you must take someone else. Take my new sealed-bottle girl. Have you ever had a sealed bottle? I will make a good price for you."

He thought rapidly. What could he do? If he were simply to leave he would never get to Munni. She would almost certainly be whisked away to another house in Kamatipura, or even out of Bombay altogether, now that Saroja knew a police investigator had got as far along the trail as he had done. So the only thing to do was to stay on.

And he had been left just one way of doing that.

"Why, yes," he said, managing a fearful smirk. "A sealed-bottle girl, that I have never had. I would very much like. Yes. Yes."

He hoped to God he had enough money on him. A virgin, even a fake one as was most likely, would not come cheap. And Saroja's "good price" was surely no more than an empty promise.

Then what if, while he was going through the pretence of being with his expensive buy, the eunuch immediately smuggled Munni out of the house? Well, it was another risk. But, yet more than before, it was a risk that he had to take. At least shut away with the sealed-bottle girl he would be able to question her, and if he went about it carefully he could perhaps find out just whereabouts in the house Munni was being kept. With luck then he could creep out and get to her. Ten minutes with her should be enough. Five even. And after all Saroja would not be keen to leave her premises with the girl while business was at its most active.

Yes, a risk worth taking.

Still smirking hard, he followed the *hijra* up the stairs out of the hall and along a wide corridor with a curtained doorway off to either side. From behind one of these as he passed he heard a plaintive male voice exclaiming, "My glasses. Where are my glasses?"

The doorway at the end of the corridor on the left had, in place of a curtain, a wooden door with a keyhole.

Was there, somewhere else not far away, a similar room with a door that could be locked? And was Munni being kept behind it?

Saroja took a key from the bunch at his waist, fitted it into the keyhole in the door in front of him, turned it.

"Go in, go in, Inspector Sahib," he said, pushing the door wide. "You would find this one everything you could wish. A real first-time girl, all for you."

Ghote walked past him into the room. He heard Saroja swiftly pull back the door and the click of the key as he relocked it. But that he had expected. And the door looked flimsy enough for him to be able, if he needed to, to force his way out.

He took in the room in one swift glance. There was no window and not much space for any furniture other than the bed and a narrow dressing table on which stood a water jug and a basin. Above that there hung a photograph, framed. It showed a girl in a graduate's gown and mortar-board cap. No doubt it was there to impress clients of the regular user of the room.

But it was the little, fragile creature lying half-asleep on her side on the inner edge of the bed dressed in a skimpy red cotton frock open at the back who drew his full attention. The sealed-bottle girl.

She looked hardly as old as his own Ved. And, though he was almost certainly not the first client to be shown into her, despite Saroja's talk, she still had all the appearance, as she turned and sat up, of a girl who had no idea what the business was all about. On her cheek he could see the indentation left by her single glass bangle on which she must have been lying as she had slept.

He gave her as reassuring a smile as he could manage and sat down cautiously on the nearest corner of the bed.

"What is your name?" he asked.

"It is Shammo."

"Shammo. That is a very nice name."

The girl nodded solemn, silent agreement.

"How long have you been here, Shammo?"

"Five days, six days. A long time."

"Yes. How did you come to be here?"

"My *ma* brought me," Shammo replied, as if it was the most natural thing in the world. "We are very poor. Sometimes there is only some tea and a banana to eat all day. My *baap* was killed when a truck fell over that he was bringing to Bombay. So we came here also because my uncle is here and my *ma* thought there would be more to eat. But it was not like that, and my baby brother was always very hungry."

"I see. But do you know why you are here? What it is for?"

"Oh yes, yes."

There was a sudden, altogether unexpected spark of eagerness in her voice.

"Yes?" Ghote asked.

"It was some time past," the girl said. "One day an old man who lived near where we were in our hut on the pavement said he would give me fifty paisa if I would do something. I did not know what that was, but I asked my *ma* and she told me what men like. So I went with him and I gave the fifty paisa to my *ma*. Then she said to me that the man had told her where to go to get many, many rupees if I would let men do the things they do. So we came here."

Ghote sat in silence on the corner of the bed. Of course, what Shammo had told him was an account of a clear breach of the law. But, bad though it was, it happened often enough. And, young though Shammo was, she did not seem horrified by what had befallen her. Perhaps he did not need to complicate his inquiry by taking up her case.

He thought all the same he ought to ask one more question.

"And men have come to you here?"

"Oh yes, yes. That is why I am in the house. They come and they do the things they want and then they go away. Are you here to do those things too?"

"But—but what do you feel? Do you mind them?"

"Sometimes, when they hurt a little. But that is nothing. My *ma* has so much of rupees now, and while they are hurting I think about other things."

"What things?"

"The game I am playing before they came, something like that."

"I see."

Ghote sighed. He had learnt in the clearest terms of a tragedy. Of yet one more victim of the cruel life of Bombay. But he was here with a different object. To stop a maniac killer.

"Tell me," he said, "do you see the other girls that are here?"

"Yes, yes. Sometimes they play with me, and I help them when they are getting ready for the evening."

"Good, good. And do you know their names?"

"Yes, I know them all. There is Sita and Akka and Parvati and Prema and—and—and there is Munni. She has not been here long. She is very nice. And there is Abida and Rekha—"

"Munni?" Ghote asked, tense as a sitar string. "Do you know where she is?"

"Where she is now?"

"Yes, yes."

"Yes, she is with a man."

"With a man, you are sure? Not hidden away somewhere?"

"No. I heard. She is having a double-extra. That man will be there all the time till morning."

"And where? Where will they be?"

"In the first place, the first on this side."

Ghote rose slowly from the bed. His limbs felt stiff.

"Thank you, Shammo," he said. "And I must go now."

"But first you must give me the money," Shammo answered. "You have to give, even if you did nothing. It is fifty rupees because I am sealed bottle."

"I see."

He fished out his wallet. Yes, he could just, by luck, manage fifty rupees. For this unsealed sealed bottle.

He handed Shammo the money, took out his penknife and with one good jerk forced open the door.

10

Carefully pulling to the broken door of Shammo's room, Ghote looked quickly along the corridor towards the archway leading down to the brothel's hall. No one appeared to be coming up. He listened hard. There were murmurs of talk from behind the curtains of the cubicles, an occasional muffled laugh, a squeak of feigned pleasure or dismay. But, as far as he could make out, none of the customers was on the point of emerging.

Quickly, but quietly as he could, he made his way towards the cubicle where, Shammo had said, Munni had taken her all-night client.

He made up his mind as he went that, whatever might seem to be going on behind Munni's curtain, he was going to walk in and get hold of her. Her customer might always turn out to be aggressive, but he doubted if he would be. Most people caught in such circumstances were likely to slide away as quickly as they could.

At the cubicle curtain he did for a moment, however, stand and listen. He heard a low insistently muttering male voice. Then a sharp instruction in Bombay Hindi, "Behave properly."

Was that Munni? It could be.

He swished back the curtain.

A man was sitting on the edge of the bed, still dressed in pure white *kurta* and many-folded *dhoti,* still even with his white Gandhi cap on his almost bald head above two thick coils of neck fat. And the girl on the bed, who had apparently resented some particularly extraordinary proposal, was not Munni.

"Munni?" Ghote barked out, balked rage flooding through him. "Where is she? Why isn't she here?"

The girl on the bed looked at him without rancour.

"Oh, she has gone," she said.

"Gone? Gone? Where gone?"

"I do not know. All I know is Saroja went to her just a little time ago and made her come away. The customer was very angry, but Saroja said he need not pay. Saroja said that even. And then Ragu, who keeps out the police and diseased men at the door, took Munni with him."

"Where to? Where to?"

"I am not knowing. Saroja was whispering only."

Ghote let the cubicle's curtain fall. As he went towards the stairs leading into the hall he heard the girl saying to her disturbed client in English, "No, no, nothing to mind. Just be happy go lucky. Just be happy go lucky."

Then abruptly the eunuch madam appeared at the foot of the stairway. Ghote acted at once.

In a moment he was facing him, placing himself squarely so that the creature had his back to the wall.

"Now," he said, "you have sent away Munni. Where have you sent?"

The hard-faced man-woman looked back at him, expression quite unchanged despite the fierceness of the challenge. Again he was assailed by a strong sweet whiff of almond oil.

"Who is Munni?" the *hijra* said.

"No. That would not do. You know full well who is the girl. She has been here for the past ten days, ever since Heera in Falkland Road sent her to you."

"Heera? What Heera is that?"

"Listen, I know that Munni has been here. You made a bad mistake in not giving her a new name."

"The bitch would not take."

Ghote drew in a deep satisfied breath. At least he had extracted some sort of an admission.

"Very well," he demanded again, "where have you sent her now? She was taken by that *goonda* you have at the door. Where did you tell him to go with her?"

"Nowhere."

He raised his hand and slapped the creature hard across the face. He stood just where he was, unflinching.

"Where?"

"If Ragu is running away with one of my girls, how should I be knowing where he has gone?"

He longed to slap him again. Harder. But from the way he had taken the first blow it was obvious that there was nothing to be got out of him like that.

He thought for a moment.

"All right," he said, "I have reason to believe you have committed an offence under Indian Penal Code Section 361, kidnap of a minor girl. You will accompany me to Nagpada Police Station where you would be charged accordingly."

"No, Inspector," Saroja replied.

"No? What are you meaning 'No'?"

"So much of *hafta* I am paying those fellows at Nagpada from top to bottom, you think I can be charged there? Rupees fifty I am giving down to rupees two, each and every week. They would laugh only, Inspector."

Ghote considered.

It was true enough that a good deal of *hafta* was paid by madams and pimps, even if not as much as Saroja had boasted of. But certainly he must have paid plenty to someone at the Nagpada station to be as sure as he was that he himself would find things made difficult if he did march him off there. And—it came to him in a dart of revelation —who would Saroja have paid his top-price fifty rupees a week to but Sub-Inspector D'Silva.

So the thing to do was not to drag the eunuch to the station now and risk a rebuff. It was to get hold of D'Silva as soon as he could, scare the living daylights out of him and then, if the *hijra* still proved obstinate, take the creature along when he could be made to see that a charge would stick.

In that way he would learn where Munni was to be found, and then perhaps he would be near at last to securing the two hundred percent proof the A.C.P. had insisted on.

In the meantime it would be as well to conceal from this half-man half-woman that he was not beaten yet.

He planted an exaggerated expression of baffled fury onto his face.

"We would see if you can be charged or not," he ground out. "We would see. All in good time."

He turned on his heel, marched through the brothel hall—custom was beginning to fall off—and stamped out.

Breathing in the cool night air of winter, he thought that Saroja ought to be feeling confident now that he had thwarted any pursuit of Munni on behalf of his friend fat Heera of Falkland Road.

It was not until next morning that Ghote was able to put into operation his plan to cut off Saroja's retreat. Arriving at the Nagpada station at an early hour he was happy to find that Sub-Inspector D'Silva was already there on duty.

"Ganesh, how are you this morning? Pretty wrecked you look, man. Saroja's girls know their business okay."

"Well, I am thinking it is Saroja herself, or himself, who knows the business."

"Himself? So you caught on, did you? Try a feel, was it? Found everything not just what you expected, eh?"

"I found what I might have expected, S.I. I found a eunuch madam paying very much of *hafta* to a police officer."

D'Silva did not seem put out, uncompromising though Ghote's tone had been.

"Yeah," he answered, "Saroja knows where his chapattis are buttered all right, and he doesn't make any difficulties about paying up."

"So he can safely keep his twelve-year-old bluff of a sealed-bottle girl?" Ghote said.

"As many as he wants, if he pays."

"Although it is an offence under I.P.C. Section 361, S.I.?"

D'Silva grinned.

"Because it's an offence, *bhai,*" he answered. "Wouldn't be worth a paisa if it wasn't breaking the law, would it? But you're not getting so stiff-necked as old Inspector D'Sa, are you, Ganesh, old friend?"

"I am not getting so much of old friend," Ghote answered. "I have come to tell you something, S.I."

"What's that, man? Don't take it all to heart like that."

"I have come to tell you that you will not allow Saroja to believe he cannot be charged under Section 361."

"But he can't, man. What else does he pay out for?"

"He is going to find that, however much he has paid out, it will be of no help to him."

"Hell, man. You got to keep your word in this game. If it gets round you don't do what you're paid for, you won't ever collect. That's the short and long of it."

"But nevertheless, S.I., this time you are not going to do what he has been paying you for."

"Old D'Sa has really got inside of you, Inspector. Live in the real world for a short time, man. You can't do things like that."

"But I am going to."

D'Silva still did not look all that upset. He hopped up to sit on the corner of his desk and gave Ghote a cheerful smile.

"Who's to make me do anything, man?"

"I am, Sub-Inspector."

"Just how would you be doing that, then?"

Ghote looked at him.

"By reporting the business at that Nariman Point flat last night to the Anti-Corruption Bureau," he said.

"But you can't do that," said D'Silva.

"I can," said Ghote.

There was a long silence. Through the windows of the police station came the sounds of busy Bombay, traffic grinding and hooting, the croaking caws of crows disputing over scraps, voices raised in loud talk and the twang-twang-twang of a passing *pinjari* advertising his willingness to tease out cotton mattresses with his single-string harp-like instrument.

"What you want exactly, Inspector?" D'Silva said at last.

"Just for you to let Saroja know that he could find himself in prison if he does not cooperate with me," Ghote said. "If you would go along there now, S.I., I can come after some time in my turn."

So before another hour had passed Ghote was making his way into the sixteen Kamatipura lanes with precise directions for finding the place to which little Munni had been hurried off the night before. He took with him the comforting assurance that Saroja had been plainly too shaken at last to have any idea about getting a warning to Munni's new *gharwali* ahead of his own visit. Indeed he was ready to bet that the *hijra* would not even admit to Heera in Falkland Road that he had let her down. Why should he?

The scene in Kamatipura at this hour of the morning was very unlike its night-time guise when the air all around had seemed to pulsate with mingled counter-currents of emotion and darts of half-released energy. Now the area was little different from any other part of lower-class Bombay, a picture of desultory domestic activity.

Children were playing everywhere. Tiny tots, naked all bar a good-luck string crossing wobbling pot-bellies, staggered from one point to another intent on their desperately serious business. A group of bigger boys was, of course, playing cricket, their wicket not three stumps topped by bails but a pile of rocks, their bat an almost formless chunk of wood. Little girls in frocks with the backs left open for coolness now that the sun was beginning to get high in the sky stood or sat in clumps, already gossiping as hard as their mothers and grandmothers.

Outside the huts that lined the lane which he had entered charpoys had been pulled into the open on either side, giving the thoroughfare the appearance of a long gappy mouth lined with irregular teeth. On most of the beds girls lay dozing after the activities of the night before. *Gharwalis* sat, almost always well fleshed and heavy, at the entrances of the huts looking down on the passing show and exchanging shouted comments on the scares and successes of the night before. A pair of goats tied to the leg of one of the charpoys had somehow scrambled up on to it and were dipping and tumbling on its stretched ropework, bleating furiously. Scrawny chickens everywhere scratched and pecked.

At the single standpipe in the lane a prostitute was bathing, the water making her thin cotton sari transparent. Her pimp or perhaps lover was sitting on a large stone not far away lazily looking at her as he puffed at a leaf-rolled *bidi*.

Ghote caught a sharp whiff of its acrid smoke as he went by.

He stopped for a moment and counted up the shacks along the lane to make sure he had the right one in his sights. And, to his delight, no sooner had he checked than he saw coming waddling out of its doorway a woman who could only be the *gharwali* of the place. As she turned and pulled the hut's door closed he noted that though she was not as massively sprawling as Heera in Falkland Road she was good and fat none the less, fat with a compacted hardness that spoke of the disciplinarian.

She had on her arm an empty basket and was no doubt off to the nearest shops to stock up with provisions for the day. Ghote stood where he was and waited for her, pretending to search in his pockets for something, a cigarette, a coin for some purchase, so as to get a good look at her as she passed him.

The glance he took only confirmed his first impression. A hard woman. Hard in body, hard in face. The upper lip between her two solid cheeks bore a distinct moustache and her straggling hair was iron-grey. From the baleful expression in her eyes he thought that whatever shopkeepers she was on her way to buy from were going to have sharp and unrewarding bargaining sessions.

As soon as she was four or five yards past he set out again, taking care not to move any more quickly than the other idle people in the lane where his clean shirt and trousers were already liable to draw unwanted attention to himself. When he reached the hut the *gharwali* had left he saw that its door was not only shut, in contrast to those of almost every other hut in the lane, but that it was also padlocked.

He stepped up and gave the dangling lock a tentative twist. It did not yield.

The experiment reinforced his belief that behind the door little Munni was to be found. No doubt Saroja would have sent with her a message to the *gharwali* here to say that she should not be allowed out at all.

Well, the whole door was a pretty second-class construction, only a few thin, warped planks, one already beginning to come away, held together by three cross-bars. A couple of good kicks and it would cease to present an obstacle.

He stood back and glanced left and right along the lane. No one was near. He raised his foot. Thank goodness he was wearing his shoes and not a pair of *chappals*.

Then, just as he was about to launch himself forward, there came from inside the shack a screech of tearing wood and the wide plank that was already half-free from the bottom-most cross-bar was heaved back from the inside. The next moment a woman's head, the dark hair dishevelled, appeared in the gap.

Munni? Was it Munni escaping? What a piece of luck that he had got here just in time.

But a second later he realised that the woman forcing her way out was nothing like little plump Munni. As she turned her shoulders and began wriggling further through he saw that she was a few years older and physically altogether a different type. Where Munni was chubby and bursting with unsuppressible vitality the young woman now crawling forward on her hands while she squirmed to get her hips through the gap in the door was lean almost to the point of gauntness and the single glimpse he had had of her face had shown him wide, staring eyes, projecting cheekbones and thin contorted lips.

So far, he realised, the girl had not seen that anyone was standing so close. But now as, her hips clear, she twisted round to get to her feet their eyes met.

At once a look of sheer terror came into the woman's face. Her thin-lipped mouth opened wide and looked as if it would never be closed again. Such colour as she had in her dark-complexioned face faded to instant greyness.

"It is all right," he said to her. "It is all right. Don't be afraid. I am not going to stop you."

Crouching on the dusty ground at his feet she looked up at him unbelievingly.

"It is all right," he repeated. "I will do nothing to stop you. You are trying to get away from this place, isn't it? Well, go. Go."

Slowly she rose to her feet. She seemed to have hurt her left leg in scraping her way through the door and as she put weight on it she lurched heavily to one side.

He put out a hand to steady her and found the arm he held was trembling with tenseness.

"You have been kept here by force?" he asked, more to provide further reassurance than because he wanted to know.

In answer the girl gave one huge air-sucking sob. And then, breaking his hold, she flung herself down at his feet and wrapped her two thin arms tightly round his thighs.

"Save me, save me," she gulped out. "Save me. Take me away from here."

A wave of coldness descended on him. What was he being asked to do? Begged to do? Plainly this was a young woman who in some way or another must have been tricked into prostitution, and she had seized the moment when her disciplinarian *gharwali* had left the hut to make this attempt at escape. Surely he would not when little Munni was there in the hut still, there with all that she could tell him. With as much gentleness as possible in the circumstances Ghote tried to release the gaunt young woman's arms from round his legs.

"Look," he said, "if you are wanting to get away you must go at once. I have seen your *gharwali*. She is on her way to buy from some shops. But I do not think she would be long. She was carrying only a small basket. So you must hurry. Come, go now."

But every time he succeeded in releasing one tight-clutching hand he found the other fiercely clamped to his trouser leg. He grew impatient.

Could he shout out to Munni in the hut, see if she would come out the way the girl had done? But that would be to draw yet more attention than the creature at his feet was already doing. In a minute or two other *gharwalis* would be coming to take their absent sister's part.

"Stop," he said to the clutching girl, raising his voice as much as he dared. "You must go. I cannot help you. I have business here. Important business."

"No," she answered, desperation choking her. "No, you are a sahib. You can help. You must. You must. I cannot do any more."

As she said these last words he realised that they were most probably exactly true. The trembling he had noticed when he had first held her arm as she had swayed and nearly fallen was more than the effect of mere fright. She was racked with fever. Her wide bloodshot eyes and heat-dried face confirmed it.

"You are ill?" he asked.

"Yes, yes. For three days I have had fever. And now I cannot move. I cannot."

With a dull certainty like a muffled hammer-stroke, he saw that she was in no way lying to him. Alone she would not be able to do more than drag herself a few yards along the lane. The *gharwali* would find her as soon as she came back. Her bid for freedom would come to nothing.

Unless indeed he himself did help her.

"Sahib," she said, her hot breath striking up at him as he leant over her. "Sahib, I come all the way from Dhadgaon village in Dhule District. My name is Lakshmi. I have been married one year only. My husband very much loved me."

She gave a harsh dry sob at that, and Ghote thought that, had she not been so strongly gripped by fever, tears would have flowed and flowed.

"My husband loved me when I was with him," she went brokenly on. "But now . . . now . . ."

"Where is your husband?" Ghote asked, at once wishing he had not let himself get further entangled.

"He is at home. He is a farmer. We were very happy. He liked me so much that even when I was talking to other women he would call me back. Then one day when I was at the bazaar with what we had to sell some women friends I had made there and a man asked me to go with them to a picture in the town. They said I could reach to home before my husband came back from the fields. But instead they took me to Nasik."

Ghote looked back along the lane in the direction that the moustached, solid-cheeked *gharwali* had taken. If only the shopkeepers she went to would be tough enough over the bargaining to delay her a little longer.

"Try to get up, Lakshmi," he said to the desperate creature at his knees.

She made no effort to comply.

"Sahib," she said, "you must help. When I found those friends were not at all friends I wept and wailed to go home. I saw a policeman and called to him. But they said I was a madwoman and they were taking me to Bombay. The policeman helped them to get me on the train. And in Bombay they sold me to Lalitabai here for rupees three hundred. Then when I refused to go with the men who came to me she gave me a harsh beating each time. And at last I obeyed. But, sahib, what if at home my husband has stopped waiting for me? What if he has already taken another wife?"

"But your husband will not have taken a new wife," Ghote said. "He loved you. You told me that. He wanted always to have you by his side when he was at home. He will not have forgotten you so soon."

"Sahib, if he has I will drown myself in that sea that I saw just once when they brought me to Bombay."

Somehow this simple declaration decided Ghote. He could not leave the creature to be found again by her brutal *gharwali* or to end her days in that grey heaving sea she had had a single sight of in all her life.

Surely if he did what he could for her as quickly as possible, took her to Bombay Central station and put her on a train for Nasik, gave her a little money, he would be able to get back here and make contact with Munni before the *gharwali* learnt he had been responsible for stealing away her three-hundred-rupee buy.

"Come," he said to Lakshmi, "I will help you as much as I can. Can you walk a little way to where I would find a taxi?"

"Yes, yes. You must help. I can walk. I must. I will."

Almost clawing her way up his body she managed to get to her feet. Then, having placed one of her arms across his shoulder, he began to walk her back along the lane in the direction of Bellassis Road where with any luck there would be a cruising taxi and further along which in any case Bombay Central station stood.

But it became evident almost at once that there would be no question of Lakshmi walking as far as the station. She was plainly very ill. The trembling that affected arms, legs and her whole body was so strong that Ghote himself at times shook with it.

He peered along the lane in the direction of the hooting, roaring traffic of Bellassis Road. Once there, they would at least be hidden from the vengeful *gharwali* by the crowds on the busy pavements while he looked about for a taxi.

But he never reached Bellassis Road.

There, coming towards them from a completely unexpected direction, marching steadily onwards, was the *gharwali*. She was still far enough off not to have seen them, and Ghote at once swung round with Lakshmi and set off back the way they had come.

They would have much farther to go now before reaching the anonymity of a crowded main street, Foras Road or perhaps Falkland Road, but there was nothing else for it. Yet would Lakshmi be able to move quickly enough to have got past the hut again before the *gharwali* caught up with them? And if she could, would they have got clear away before she discovered her loss?

"Try to walk faster," he urged Lakshmi, steering her round a man hammering out gilt buttons on a bench outside his dark hut of a workshop.

But his words had the opposite effect from what he had intended. Lakshmi came to an abrupt halt.

"No more," she moaned. "Let her come. No more."

Ghote felt a hard stream of rage jet out of him. No, dammit, he had not risked missing Munni and her precious information just to have this wretched creature be caught again almost outside the very hut they had started from.

He seized her arm in a grip that took no account of her condition and propelled her onwards, even managing to break into a shambling half-run with her.

They passed the hut and for a hundred yards more kept on at the same stumbling pace. The junction of Foras Road and Falkland Road came into sight, not two hundred yards further on. The sound of the traffic there, bus horns grunting, scooter horns parping, was music in Ghote's ears.

But then, over the sound of the music, he heard a shrill indignant cry.

"Stop! Stop! Stop!"

The *gharwali*. She must have reached her hut, have realised in a moment or been told by busy gossiping neighbours what had happened and now—he glanced back—she was coming after them, advancing along the lane at a slow but implacably determined run.

He took a better hold of Lakshmi's arm and broke into a run of his own once more. But the girl was like a dead weight beside him, a lifeless bale of rags.

Staggering pace by staggering pace they went towards the noise and bustle of the crossroads and possible safety. But each lunge forward seemed to Ghote to be harder to make than the lunge before.

He took another look back. The *gharwali* was barely twenty yards away.

And she had probably seen his face, he realised. Even if he could haul the dead weight of Lakshmi as far as the two intersecting main roads ahead, even if in the crowd there they managed to conceal themselves, that moustached brute might well know him again.

Was his way to Munni blocked once more then?

But he could not bring his brain to deal with any future problem. Every part of his will was needed to drag and heave forwards the sick kidnapped creature by his side.

But Lakshmi, too, had looked back and seen the *gharwali* so close behind and the sight of that countenance, so filled with unforgiving rage, had quite a different effect on her than it had done a few minutes before when she had begged him to stop their flight. Now a sudden access of fear and fear-driven energy seized her.

It was she who dragged Ghote on now. Holding his arm in a grip that almost stopped the flow of blood in it, she put her head down and dived towards safety.

Then at last they were at the crossroads. And people, people marvellously densely crowded together, were all in front of them.

"Stop! Stop!"

Ghote cast another glance behind.

The *gharwali* seemed to have found new strength. She was running faster than before, and only some ten or twelve yards separated them now.

Could they after all fail to hide from her? How much more had she seen of his face?

He forced his weary legs into yet fiercer action.

Harder now by a great deal to make progress. The crowd, which he had seen as their salvation, was providing a series of infuriating obstacles. Diving sideways to get round a little boy hanging with one hand on to his mother's sari while the thumb of his other was jammed into his mouth, Ghote was forced to come to a full check because the whole outer edge of the pavement was occupied by a spice seller with his piles of powders in neat cones spread all over a large white cloth and a transistor radio beside him bleating out a *filmi* song.

He sneaked another look back. The *gharwali* was almost within reaching distance. And then a splendid gap opened up in the crowd in front of him and, heaving Lakshmi forwards, he knew he had widened the distance between them and their pursuer once again.

That chance to make progress had dictated which of the two busy streets at the junction they took. Falkland Road.

With a sudden curiously hollow feeling Ghote realised that if they succeeded in keeping ahead of the *gharwali* for a few minutes more they would actually pass the house where, that fatal night, he had had his glimpse of a too well-known face.

If only he had not . . . How much easier his life would be if he were still simply dealing with the chain-snatching case at the City Light Cinema.

The traffic on the roadway beside them mysteriously eased off and in an instant he dragged Lakshmi, who no longer seemed to know what was happening to her, off the pavement. Now at last he could really set some distance between them and the *gharwali*.

Surely, fat as she was, she would before much longer have to give up the chase? But the expression of fixed determination he had seen each time he had looked back could well mean otherwise.

A handcart, long as a boat and as slow to steer, came noisily trundling up behind them, the man pushing it at a run calling out, "Way please, way please," with every breath. Ghote leapt for the pavement again, hauling Lakshmi after him. His hand circling her waist could feel the fevered blood in her body, hot to the touch.

Another quick look back. And another, more distant sight of that implacable moustached face forcing its way through the throng.

And then, abruptly, above the swaying, bobbing mass of shining black heads in front of him he saw something familiar and, he felt at once, warmly reassuring. The bright red painted sign outside Dr. Falli Framrose's dispensary, *Sex Diseases, Sex Changes*.

That would be the answer. To take Lakshmi in there. If Dr. Framrose was present . . . If only he was not wandering about the area as he had been at their last encounter . . . A doctor. A doctor was what Lakshmi needed. And, if things went luckily for them, they might succeed in dodging in at his door without the *gharwali* seeing where they had gone.

He bent to his task of lugging Lakshmi onwards with a new determination. A man with a goatskin bag of water: dodge round him. A man with a harmonium on his head, evidently playing music in his imagination and failing to look where he was going: a slide to the left, pushing poor Lakshmi hard, and that obstacle was dealt with. A boy darting out from an Irani café carrying six glasses of tea, three in the fingers of each hand: brush past him with a swerve, spilling his precious load no doubt, but this was no time to be punctilious.

And then Dr. Framrose's door. Open.

One more look back. The man with the harmonium had come into collision with the *gharwali* and had forced her to a standstill. She was abusing him swiftly and ferociously. He was abusing her back.

In at the doorway. Drag Lakshmi after him. Let her slide to the floor, exhausted.

Sanctuary.

11

Ghote found Dr. Framrose every bit as helpful as he had hoped. The eccentric Parsi grasped the situation as quickly as Ghote could explain it, and at once, sending Ghote himself to keep watch on the street in case the vengeful *gharwali* contrived to find out from idlers nearby where her quarry had gone, he went to his locked drugs cupboard and looked for whatever medication would soonest benefit the almost unconscious Lakshmi.

By the time Ghote had satisfied himself that the *gharwali* had been entirely thwarted the doctor had treated Lakshmi and got her onto a cot at the back of his premises.

"So, my dear fellow," he said, turning from washing his hands at the basin in his front room, "are we to see you bringing a case against the woman who so mistreated my patient? There are marked signs of injuries to the dorsal region inflicted over a considerable period."

Ghote found the innocent inquiry difficult to answer. He could not tell the doctor that he had more important inquiries to make which would prevent his taking action over Lakshmi. The Parsi had shown himself only too full of curiosity before, and would be bound to want to know just what these inquiries were. In no time the Sheriff of Bombay's forbidden name would be on the verge of being spoken.

"Well, we would have to see," he contented himself with answering. "It is not always easy to get proper evidence in such cases, you understand."

Dr. Framrose laughed his high-pitched laugh.

"Money will change hands at some stage, no doubt," he said. "Nothing in this life is free from that distorting influence, my good Inspector. Especially not when matters of a sexual nature are involved."

Ghote saw at once that he had been given an excellent opportunity of heading the talk away from the danger area. A little philosophising would be much to the doctor's taste, he guessed.

He wagged his head with a deprecating smile.

"Ah, Doctor Sahib," he said, "I am thinking that the activities of the part of the city where you are working have given you too much of a sour view of life. Surely money does not enter into each and every sexual matter."

"But it does, my dear fellow. It does."

Thank goodness, the fellow was off, riding a hobby horse as if he was thundering a winner to the post at Mahalaxmi racecourse.

"Consider the average middle-class matrimonial arrangement in India, my dear chap. There is a boy with a career of some sort, with a certain salary and certain prospects. There is a girl, possessed of certain physical attractions and with parents ready to provide a dowry of certain dimensions, despite the provisions of the Dowry Act under which dowry, of course, no longer exists. Correct so far?"

"Quite correct, I suppose, Doctor Sahib."

"Very well. Negotiations take place. And what is the ultimate outcome? That the lady in question sells her body for a sum to be paid in instalments over a lifetime. Not different in essence from the transactions that take place in Falkland Road here every night of the year."

Ghote thought for a moment of his own marriage. True, he did support Protima and also had sexual relations with her. Yet the doctor's view of the situation did not seem somehow at all to describe what actually took place between them.

"Well, I am able to see your point of view, Doctor," he answered. "But all the same I think it is not always exactly as you are making out, if I may say it."

"Ah well, perhaps not absolutely always, my friend. Perhaps I do exaggerate somewhat at times. I admit it. I see myself, you know, as a scourge, a scourge of the age, and I never like to subtract from that romantic image."

"I understand," Ghote said.

But he did not. He had grasped the doctor's concept of a "romantic image," but he was not at all sure what exactly the English word "scourge" meant. It teased at his mind, but the doctor's continuing excited flow left him no moment to fish for it.

"No, no, I assure you, my friend, things are as I have described them. Witnessing the activities that go on all around me here I can hold no other views. None. The exchange of coinage, the offering of favours. That is all that it amounts to, and it goes on and on and on."

Something in the fellow's tone, his wild belittling of all human conduct, now abruptly sent a seeping flood of depression through Ghote's mind. Was the world really as bad as that? It was hard to fight against the notion. Here he was himself, not an hour ago filled with hope, sure that at last he was on the point of bringing to justice a man seemingly above the law, and in just that short time he had been reduced to impotence.

True, in helping Lakshmi to escape he had beaten the Kamatipura lane *gharwali*. But at what a cost. The creature had had sight of his face more than once. She would almost certainly know him again. If he were to go now and attempt to see Munni in that shack he would be recognised at once, if not as a policewalla at least as an interferer, an enemy. He would never be able, use what wiles he might, to get near the little plump prostitute. And the knowledge that she was likely to possess.

Was his inquiry at an end then? Already? Was the crusade he had fought to be allowed to carry on to be cut off like this?

Gloom swirled around him.

He ceased to listen to the doctor's continued outpouring, the philosophising which he had a moment earlier been so pleased with himself for provoking.

Then, like a shaft of sun breaking through a hitherto unnoticed rift in massively piled dark monsoon clouds, a thought came to him.

Munni was not the only way to get evidence against the Sheriff. If the Sheriff had killed Kamla by strangling her with that whip, had he not also killed another girl, Veena Bhaskar the student, in just the same fashion? Was it not the very similarity in the modus operandi in each case that had made him so determined that the fellow must be stopped, however influential he was? Well then, get at him from this other angle.

His course was clear. Examine the full particulars of the Veena Bhaskar case and interview those most closely connected with it. Perhaps then some fact would emerge that might point directly to the Sheriff. Whoever was in charge of the Bhaskar case could not possibly recognise the significance of some such chance detail. Only he himself, with his knowledge that it was the Sheriff who had been in the

Falkland Road brothel at the time of Kamla's murder, was in a position to spot any link between the two affairs. Very well, he would set out to do just that.

Immediately.

"But, Doctor Sahib," he interrupted blatantly, "I must not stand here all the day talking. A police officer has his duties you know. So may I please come later and send back that poor girl in the next room to her waiting husband, and in the meanwhile I would go about my business."

"Certainly, certainly, my dear fellow," the doctor said, cheerfully dismissing the rudeness of the interruption. "Go out by all means. Arrest a few more murderers. Halt a few more black-money deals. Put an end to corruption all over Bombay. The day is young still. You have time. You have time."

Ghote had seen himself interviewing first most probably the parents of the student who had been killed in a fashion so horribly similar to that in which Kamla had died. He would be, to all outward appearances, merely carrying out the parallel investigation of a serious offence which Crime Branch often undertook superimposed upon regular inquiries in whatever area of the city an offence had taken place. But when he came to acquaint himself with the details of the affair he met with a distinct surprise.

Veena Bhaskar, post-graduate student in sociology, had, it appeared been working in the days immediately before her death as an assistant to a visiting American professor. And that professor's name, Ghote learnt with a feeling of dismaying unreality, was Dr. Ringelnatz.

There could hardly be, he thought, two Dr. Ringelnatzes in Bombay. Could there even be two in America?

So the Sheriff's second victim had been helping the foreign lady sociologist whom he had encountered in Falkland Road in such embarrassing circumstances when he had taken the Svashbuckler on that tour of the Cages which had ended so disastrously.

In a roundabout way then he himself was responsible for Veena Bhaskar's death. Plainly the Sheriff must have spotted her at some time as she had gone to and fro in Kamatipura with that extraordinary American lady, taking notes of the customs and procedures of the district, acting as interpreter and guide.

He had not thought for a moment, when he had urged Dr. Ringelnatz to find someone to accompany her and thus avoid incidents like the abuse, and worse, she had had hurled at her from an upper window that night, that she would choose anyone but a man, a man even of a certain age, as her companion. But she had taken Veena Bhaskar—What was it the girl was known as? Yes. Sweetie—And Sweetie Bhaskar had all too evidently caught the Sheriff's eye somewhere one night in Kamatipura and had thus met her death.

So the obvious person to interview was Dr. Ringelnatz herself. Perhaps she would even be able to tell him she had been with Sweetie Bhaskar when a man, whom she might identify as the Sheriff, had spoken to the girl and had then gone off with her on some trumped-up excuse.

The way to that two hundred percent proof looked suddenly marvellously possible.

Perhaps even, he thought in his sudden ballooning of optimism, Dr. Ringelnatz as a native speaker of English and an academic person could clear up another mystery for him, a little mystery. It had niggled at him at intervals ever since his last conversation with Dr. Framrose. The exact meaning of the English word "scourge." Was a scourge some sort of plague? A scourge of rats? Was that it? Certainly Bombay suffered from a scourge of rats. They were to be seen any night you liked scampering in and out of patches of neglected ground even in the spacious, dignified area of the Fort. But had not the Parsi said that he saw himself as a scourge? Surely he would not see himself as so many rats?

Well, when he had learnt all he could about Sweetie Bhaskar from Dr. Ringelnatz perhaps he could briefly turn to that less serious matter.

He hurried away, eager to get to the university central building between the High Court and the Old Secretariat where, he had gathered from the papers on the case, Dr. Ringelnatz had been lent a cabin.

But, as he might have expected, it took him more than a little time to locate her. He inquired here, he inquired there. He was sent to one office, only to be told that he had come to quite the wrong place and must go to yet another. Only there to be sent back to the first office. A side trip to the Grand Hotel in Ballard Estate, where he remembered the American sociologist had said she was staying when he had put her into her taxi that night in Falkland Road, proved equally fruitless.

Yet each check only sharpened his feeling that Dr. Ringelnatz must have some piece of knowledge about Sweetie Bhaskar that would link her, with a link that defied any attempt at deception, to the Sheriff. The sun climbed the light blue cloudless winter sky as he marched from one part of the university building to another. It reached its zenith. It began to decline. He would have liked to have taken a break and at least have got himself a cold drink. But he did not dare. Only if he kept going, hurrying from place to place, pushing for replies, bullying clerks, flattering administrators he felt would he be sure of getting his quarry at last.

But he was fearfully thirsty. And hungry, too.

It was a little past two o'clock when, making his way to yet another doorway in the building where there was a room in which he had been told Dr. Ringelnatz was certain to be found, that he actually saw her. He almost went rushing past so determined was he in his chase.

But she was there in front of him, strolling across one of the university lawns accompanied by a very tall, bespectacled man wearing a long, high-buttoned white *sherwani,* thigh-tight *churidar pyjama* and a white turban tied in the Punjabi way.

He left the path he had been hurrying along and headed towards the short, stringy-limbed American lady, dressed it appeared in the same sun-bleached blouse and skirt that had met with such an unfortunate experience in night-time Falkland Road. But five yards from her he had to come to a halt. She was engaged in such earnest conversation that there seemed no way to break in.

Her towering Punjabi companion was in mid-flow, though Dr. Ringelnatz, from somewhere not much above his waist, kept pouncing at him with sharp comment like a diminutive dog barking at a passing buffalo.

Very little of what the Punjabi was saying was comprehensible to Ghote. It was evident that he was, like Dr. Ringelnatz, a sociologist and that the two of them were arguing out a matter concerned with their subject. It even emerged gradually as Ghote, constrained to walk backwards in front of them in the hope of catching the American lady's eye, took in phrases here and there that they were discussing the very area of life in Bombay that he was himself at this moment most interested in.

". . . Many, many of these subjects are found, you know, to be having faith in gods and goddesses even long after they have entered the brothels . . ." ". . . allowed him limited sexual liberties until . . ." ". . . thereafter he carried out full-fledged coitus . . ."

The two of them came to the edge of the lawn and as one turned to pace solemnly back. Ghote, who in his efforts to put himself fully in Dr. Ringelnatz's view had had to hop over a narrow flower-bed bordering the grass, now jumped over it again and hurried forward so as to bring himself into her line of sight once more.

"No, no, my dear madam." The tall Punjabi had paused to take in one of Dr. Ringelnatz's barked interjections. "No, no, figures are not to be obtained. You see, the Vigilante Branch of the police here, that is, the department which has in charge vice matters, keeps no records of the numbers of prostitutes. To do so would be to admit officially their existence, and that of course cannot be done."

"But you, Professor, have you not formed even a guesstimate?"

"I should say something of the order of half a lakh plus. That is, fifty thousand, perhaps sixty thousand."

"Most interesting, most interesting. Now Sprague has found—"

"Ah, Sprague, yes. Excellent research. Excellent. We apply it in our own field."

"But—"

But the Punjabi was not so easily to be stopped. The spate gushed out again and Ghote could only continue retreating in front of them in his awkward backward dance.

They reached the other end of the lawn. This time Ghote came hard up against the scaly trunk of a palm tree. The two academics wheeled round, still unnoticing.

But now Ghote felt he had had enough. The torrent of words was not ever going to leave him a gap.

"So the Indian husband, madam, is like God Almighty to the Indian wife at the beginning of the marriage period. He is not able to do wrong. He is, of necessity, perfect. But in reality you will find he frequently comes out altogether low. He goes to other women for coitus or on occasion for companionship only. But our ancient law of

Manu decrees that, though devoid of all of good qualities, the husband must yet be worshipped as a god, and therefore—"

"Excuse, please."

He had run up and planted himself slap-bang in front of them. They could not choose but pay him attention.

"Excuse, please, madam and sir, but I am a police officer and on most urgent business."

He turned to Dr. Ringelnatz.

"Madam, perhaps you are being so kind as to remember me. It is Inspector Ghote. We were meeting at Falkland Road. Madam, there was an incident."

"Oh yes, yes. Very good of you, Inspector. But quite unnecessary I assure you. In field-work of that nature some initial opposition is to be expected. And in any case all of that's been overcome now."

"Overcome, madam?"

"Yes, yes. I have an assistant, from the university here. Very good, too."

"Ah, but you have not got any more, isn't it? Miss Veena Bhaskar has unfortunately expired."

"No, no, not that silly girl. Well, mustn't speak ill of the dead, especially when she met a violent end as I understand. But she was not at all the sort of material I required. Always late, always giggling with the friend she brought along with her, some girl taking a degree in Home Science, if you please. No, no, a great mistake. My Mr. Yajnik is altogether much more satisfactory."

"I am happy to hear, madam," Ghote answered. "But, please, could you tell something of Miss Bhaskar? How many days was she with you in Kamatipura?"

"Oh, a week maybe. Something like that. Why do you ask, Inspector?"

But that Ghote was not going to tell her. Instead he put another question, his key question.

"And in that time, madam, did Miss Bhaskar meet with any persons in the vicinity? Did she attract any attention?"

"Meet any persons? Well, hell, of course she did. She met the girls I wanted to interview, when she could be persuaded to get round to it."

"No, no, madam, I am not meaning the gay—" But he remembered, vividly, the contempt his use of the expression "gay girls" had produced at their previous encounter. "I am not meaning any prostitutes, madam, but persons of the male sex. Did she meet with any of those while you were with her in Kamatipura?"

"She certainly did not," said Dr. Ringelnatz. "I had trouble enough with that Usha Wab-something-or-other. I wasn't going to have my work schedule delayed while that hussy talked to any boy-friends."

"No, madam," Ghote acknowledged. "Kindly excuse me for have interrupted your discussions."

He turned and trudged away. Behind him he heard the lofty Punjabi resume his interrupted discourse.

"The Indian husband of the middle class today wishes often his wife to be modern outside. But inside the home it is absolute orthodoxy that he requires. Such cases are galore . . ."

Ghote let the sound of the lecturing voice fade away. He felt it as an insult added to injury. Not only had his high hopes of learning from Dr. Ringelnatz that Sweetie Bhaskar had had some clear connection with the Sheriff come to nothing, but he had had to endure all that torrent of opinion.

He marched out to the wide pavement opposite the grassy stretch of the Oval Maidan with its dotted figures of cricketers and cows happily intermingled.

What to do now? The most hopeful aspect of this side of his investigation had abruptly petered out, and the Munni trail seemed equally blocked to him.

A gaggle of girl students, butterfly bright in assorted saris, brushed past him, their voices shrilly raised.

"Oh, gosh, that chap's a really sad case. You know what he tried to do to Usha? He tried to hold her hand. Yes, actually he tried that, the dashed Romeo."

Usha. The common girl's name flicked at something already almost buried in Ghote's memory. Dr. Ringalnatz had spoken of an Usha. Sweetie Bhaskar's friend, always giggling with her, like these girls just entering the university gate. Exchanging gossip about boys they knew. If Sweetie had had any dealings with the Sheriff—and she must have done if he truly was her murderer, if the coincidence of the murder method meant anything—then surely it would be to Usha . . . Usha Who? Usha Who?

Dr. Ringelnatz had mentioned the surname. He was almost sure.

He racked his brains. And piece by piece he contrived to reproduce every word of that recent hurried conversation.

Only to meet unexpected defeat. He had the answer all right. Clearly as if he had been playing a tape to himself, Dr. Ringelnatz's exact words. *I had trouble enough with that Usha Wab-something-or-other.* That, and no more, was what she had said.

Should he rush back inside the university garden, hope to find Dr. Ringelnatz still locked in discussion, demand that she search her memory for that elusive name? A moment's thought told him that it would be useless. Plainly Dr. Ringelnatz had never mastered the, to her, odd Indian name. No doubt it was one of the longer ones and so had—

No, but wait. If it was a lengthy name and if it did begin with Wab, then he had some clues. A Miss Usha Wab-something who was, yes, a Home Science student. It might be possible with luck and hard work to pinpoint her exactly from university records.

He turned back and headed for the massive old-style French portal of the building behind him.

12

Usha Wabgaonkar. It took Ghote the whole of the rest of the day to track down that name in the university registrar's stacked, softly papery-smelling files. But at last he had it. He had the girl's name—there was no other it could have been—and he had her address, a flat in the Mahim area somewhere off Lady Jamsethji Cross Road No. 2, no doubt her parents' place. He had even remembered to find out what lectures the girl was meant to attend and had discovered that she should be at home next morning.

Proceeding northwards through the city on his way to her against the unceasing incoming flow of morning traffic, he began to work out as he sat in the back of the car how he might get to talk to this giggly student Dr. Ringelnatz had so much disapproved of without either of her parents being present. If he was going to hear from her the secrets of her friend Sweetie Bhaskar's life it would be a great advantage not to have any intimidating elder presence.

They passed behind Shivaji Park and Ghote abruptly recalled the handful of dirty pictures he had hidden there in his early days in Bombay. They had not really been very dirty, he remembered, merely fuzzy shots of temple carvings from Konarak. For a few moments he was tempted to tell his driver to pull up and to leave him and enter the park. Perhaps reviving memory would guide him to the very tree into which he had thrust that dangerous little bundle of postcards. Might they really still be there? Curled strips of pasteboard, blotted to nothingness by twenty or more damp-spreading monsoons, twenty scorching summers? But no time for such nonsense. He was—surely now?—on the active track of the Sheriff of Bombay, sex murderer.

The City Light Cinema appeared on their left. Well, he had wanted to work on a more important case than that chain-snatching and his prayer had been answered. To the full.

Then, after a certain amount of craning out of the car by his driver asking directions and receiving contradictory information, they were there.

The block was clean and well kept. Ghote examined the board in the building's entrance hall, climbed two flights of stone stairs and found the Wabgaonkar flat. He rang the bell beside the name decoratively painted on a slice of varnished tree branch.

The door was opened by a girl of about twenty, as he judged. Tallish, with a rather big beaky nose but large, luminous eyes. So quite pretty. Especially in the crisp green cotton sari she was wearing. With any luck this would be Usha Wabgaonkar herself. Perhaps he could persuade her to go for a stroll while he talked to her before her mother got to know he had called.

"Miss Wabgaonkar? Miss Usha Wabgaonkar?"

"Yes? Who are you?"

She seemed a little scared. But that was perhaps natural.

He explained who he was and what he required, concisely as he could in case she did want to go out instead of speaking to him in front of a parent.

But, slightly to his surprise, she simply said at the end of his explanation, "Come in, Inspector, I will help with what I can."

"But—but perhaps you would prefer . . . Are your parents at home now?"

"No, no. I live here on my own. My mother is in Poona. My father was an Income Tax officer there."

"Ah, I see."

He followed her in, finding the flat unexpectedly well furnished. There was a carpet with a pattern of red flowers, three comfortable armchairs, a television and a telephone.

This last particularly disconcerted him. He had looked up Wabgaonkar in the directory the evening before with the intention of ringing up to make an appointment and there had been no Wabgaonkar at this address.

But perhaps the name had been omitted in error from the book, or the phone newly installed.

He shrugged.

Usha Wabgaonkar offered him tea or a cold drink. He accepted the former with quick gratitude. Nothing like a cosy chat over a cup of tea for getting the most out of an innocent person under interview. And when the main business was over perhaps he might just ask if she knew the meaning of that damned word "scourge." He had puzzled at it again during the night and had reached no satisfactory answer.

Did it mean something like "scour"? That was a word for scrubbing, wasn't it? Had Dr. Framrose meant that he saw himself scrubbing clean filthy Bombay, ridding it somehow of all the anti-socials, miscreants and riff-raffs?

It did not seem exactly right.

But no matter. Perhaps one casual question on leaving and the niggle would be dispelled.

"Now, as I told," he began comfortably when he had Usha's pretty flowered cup and saucer in his hand, "I am hoping to find from one who was Miss Veena Bhaskar's close friend anything to help my inquiries. Especially I want to know whether in her last days she had made any agreement to meet any person, any male person, who might have later been responsible for her death."

"But no, Inspector. She met no one of that sort. I am certain of that."

Ghote wagged his head.

"Ah, but a young girl like you," he said, "you cannot know enough what is like the world. I am sorry to inform you of this, but it is true that even the most respectable man in appearance can turn up to have very, very bad qualities when it is a matter of sex only."

He thought Usha must be blushing she was looking down so hard at the delicate, gold-worked *chappal* dangling half off her left foot.

"Yes, yes," he hurried on. "This is not at all a nice thing to have to talk. But it must be done. If Veena's murderer is to be found."

"Yes," Usha said, seeming to emerge from her pit of shyness. "I do want that man to be found."

"Then think again please. Did she tell at any time that she was going to meet some person, any person, you did not know?"

Usha shook her head blankly.

"There was no one," she said. "I do not think there was anyone I can tell you about, Inspector."

Ghote decided a change of tactics might bring more success. He set aside his tea and assumed a rather knowing air.

"Now, you young college girls," he said. "I am very much understanding the goings-on you modern girls are getting up to. There are boy-friends and suchlike that you do not wish your parents to be hearing about. Oh, very, very innocent, I am sure. But you young people are always thinking that the seniors have never been young themselves. It is not at all so, I can assure you. Not at all. So, please, once more will you ask yourself again?"

He had thought, as he had been speaking, that for an instant he had caught a flash of something in this rather confident girl's eyes. A hint perhaps that she had a secret.

But when she answered it was only to assure him yet again that she could think of no one.

He pressed her once more and at length, doubling his put-on air of cynicism. But he got nothing in return except an expression of the same blank inability to help. Yet, for all that the words were almost exact repetitions of what she had already said, the feeling grew on him that she was concealing something. That she did indeed have some secret.

He picked up his cup of nearly cold tea, and as he did so the sight of its pretty flowered pattern and its thinness to the touch as he put it to his lips added another factor to the tiny suspicion that he had begun to harbour.

Was not the cup of too good quality? Was not the whole flat very much better furnished than it ought to be? Surely the daughter of a former I.T. officer could hardly expect to live on her own in such a posh place as this. To have a television set, a telephone? Something was not as it should be.

He allowed himself a moment to plan his move after he had set down the empty cup. Then he rose to his feet.

"Well, Miss Wabgaonkar," he said, "I will not hide from you that I had hoped you would be of more help. But if you are knowing nothing, you are knowing nothing. I must make inquiries elsewhere."

He saw, as he had hoped to, a certain tenseness melt out of the girl with his words. He allowed her to escort him to the door of the flat.

And there he whirled round to face her.

"A whip," he snapped out. "Do you know that it was a whip that was used to kill your friend? A whip. It was pulled round her neck and tightened and tightened until she choked to death. And that was after she had been beaten with it, Miss Wabgaonkar. Flogged with it."

Yes, her face had lost its colour. She had looked all round her as if seeking urgent physical support.

"Now," he said, holding her gaze with his own, "what do you know about your friend Sweetie that you have not told to anyone? What is it? What?"

"Insp—Inspector."

Tears suddenly poured down. She turned, head lowered, almost charged back into the room and fell into one of its comfortable armchairs.

Ghote followed close behind. He reached forward, took her chin in his hand and turned her face firmly till she had to look him in the eyes again.

"Well, what? What?"

"Inspector, we—we—We went to men, Inspector. Men someone we are knowing had arranged. In hotel rooms. We—"

She broke off.

"You were call-girls?" Ghote said.

He felt astonished, even though he had sensed that the girl's flat was somehow too well furnished and had divined that she had some secret that concerned her friend as well as herself. But he had had such a fixed idea about girl students and the innocent, gossipy, giggling lives they led that the notion of any one of them acting as a prostitute, even if of a good deal higher class than the whores of Falkland Road, had not for a moment entered his head.

"Yes," Usha answered. "We were call-girls. I am one still. When you came to the door I was afraid you would be a man who had somehow learnt my true name and address. I am called Mumtaz when I am working, you know, and everything is fixed up by a man who first told me what a nice life I could lead if I wanted, instead of having to live in misery and economic stringency and all."

Her contact man, Ghote thought. Perhaps he ought to do something about putting an end to the fellow's activities, seeing him behind bars. But, again, any such action would only interfere with his present task, and that was something that must take priority. To catch a killer, a killer such as he had described to Usha, on the loose and protected by the thorn hedges of respect that surrounded such a person as the Sheriff of Bombay.

"So," he said to the girl huddled in the chair in front of him, "your friend Sweetie was meeting strange men, many strange men. Why would you not tell me that when it was one of those perhaps who killed her?"

"Inspector, I wanted to tell. But I could not. There is my way of living. Inspector, what I have wanted all the time is a respectable status. I was clever at school and was able to go to college, but there I was laughed at and all. Because I was poor, Inspector, and my father had been a clerk only in the Tax Office in Poona. And I knew that when I had got my B.A. I would be able to have nothing more than work like his, if I got work at all. Inspector, howsoever well a young girl does in an office if she is in lower ranks she is looked down upon, rebuked and snubbed. You know that is so, isn't it? Inspector, you see, I have really enjoyed being imparted love and attention by big people since I took up this line. I have lived at last, Inspector."

She looked up at Ghote fiercely. He found he had nothing to say to her.

"Please let me tell you why I came into this line," she said.

He let himself give her the merest nod of acquiescence.

"Inspector," she tumbled out, "my father, though he was poor, loved me very much but my mother was not much caring about me. I do not know why. But she never paid me much of attention. Then when I was ten years of age, I came back from school one day and I found my father was dead. He had had fever for only two days. He had said it was not bad. But then he died. And afterwards my mother would not look after me at all. So I played in the street in the new, very poor quarter where we had had to go, and I found the boys there liked to hug me and even to touch my budding breasts and fiddle me in another place. So I learnt what it is men want."

It must happen often enough, Ghote thought. It is no use pretending that children are made of sugar. Something to have remembered before starting to think of Usha as all frolicking innocence.

"And then," Usha went on, "though by taking some work I had been able to go to college, when I met that man who offered me this fine life I am having I was pleased to accept his wishes."

She looked up at him again.

"And now it all will go, isn't it, Inspector?" she said. "Isn't it?"

"We would see," Ghote answered, biting the words off. "But first you must tell everything you know about Sweetie."

"Yes, yes. I will. I will. Inspector, I had not heard. Not—not about that whip, Inspector."

"Very well. But tell me now please."

Usha took a deep breath.

"Sweetie was very different from me," she said. "Her parents are well off. Her father is in a very, very lucrative business. As a small child, she often told me, she had many, many toys, nice things to eat always and nice clothes to wear. But her parents all the same neglected her. She was put each night into a separate room to sleep while downstairs her parents were having guests all the time. They locked her in that room even, but she would get out through the bathroom and watch what they were doing, drinking alcohol, mixing freely, cutting dirty jokes and all. When she grew a little more old her mother took some notice of her. But it was only to praise her beauty, never to give praise for her achievements at school. She would say again and again, 'When you are older you will be killing and so many boys will be after you'!"

A sudden new gush of tears interrupted the account.

"Killing," Usha choked out. "And now she has been killed, killed in that horrible way. Inspector, you must nab the man who did that."

"I will," Ghote said. "I am promising that I will."

"Yes. Yes, well, when Sweetie did get old enough to come to college at first her parents went on as they did before. They gave her a big, big allowance and she used to throw parties and take alcoholic drinks and visit discos and all. And there was sex also."

Another common enough pattern, Ghote commented to himself. Or not quite so common. But it happened. And it was hard to blame the child when it did.

"Then one night," Usha said, "when Sweetie's parents were out and she had brought her friends to her house—it is on Pali Hill, like a film star's only—and there was drinking and some of those boys and girls were smoking *charas* and some had gone into another room and were indulging in some sorts of sex play, the parents unexpectedly came back. Her father, who had never given her much of attention, became very, very excited. In absolute anger he said if she ever brought home again any of those friends she would be severely punished. He stopped giving her any money, so after some time she asked me how I had begun to have money when my father was dead and my mother poor. Then she joined the call-girl line with me."

"I see," Ghote said. "But let me make it clear. Your activities, the activities both of you went in for, put you in very serious danger. It must have been through this contact man of yours that Sweetie met the person who brought about her death."

It was possible, he thought. Why should not the Sheriff have made use of a snake like that fellow to further his pleasures as well as visiting the Cages on his own?

But Usha was firmly shaking her head in negative.

"No, Inspector, no. It cannot have been like that. You see, in the time before Sweetie was killed she was not working in this line. She— Well, Inspector, she thought she had caught a disease. She had found a doctor—some lady doctor I do not know—that she could go to and who would not tell her parents. That was good. But because of what had happened to her she was not going to any men at all at that time. Not at all."

Ghote felt his hopes sinking again. He had envisaged that Usha would know the men Sweetie went to, that they were bound to have exchanged secrets. Or, failing that, her contact man would know and could be made to tell. But if what Usha had just told him was true, and there was no reason why it should not be, then Sweetie had had no appointment with the Sheriff that could be traced back.

Once again the trail was dead.

13

Ghote knew, however, that he was not going to let the whole business drop simply because there seemed to be no way forward. The thought of the Sheriff there impregnable, ready when the black impulse came over him once more to seize some poor unfortunate creature, flog her horribly and strangle her with the whip he had used, would not let him rest. Going disconsolately back south to Crawford Market Headquarters, he saw in his mind's eye again and again the Sheriff as he had been in his huge house after the meeting of the All-India Social Hygiene Samaj, standing tall and secretly amused in his den with that impudent stolen notice *Fight Immorals* presiding over everything. He heard that English sahib's voice boasting about not being Lakshman who never looked at Sita above her feet, saw the hand boldly writing that message on the glossy photograph, *To young Ved. Keep a straight bat.*

He would stop him. He would see him brought to justice. Somehow. In some way or another.

And gradually, like the first intangible tinglings of a lightning-riven monsoon storm, it was borne in on him just what next step he could take. The path leading to little Munni, Munni who had shared surely dead Kamla's secrets in the brothel in Falkland Road, was not really as blocked as he had believed.

True, that grim, grey-haired, moustached *gharwali* had seen him at close range and would in all likelihood know him again if he were to go to her hut making inquiries. But she had not seen his face for so very long. She had not exchanged a word with him, beyond shouting after him as he had hurried away dragging fever-sapped Lakshmi. It was a fair chance then that, if his appearance was not as it had been the day before, she would not recognise him.

If he went to that Kamatipura lane hut this evening in the guise of a simple low-caste customer only . . .

It had not required any nonsensical business with a false moustache or a grey-haired wig. All that had been necessary was to put on a pair of half-pants smeared with dust—Protima had unearthed the pair he used to have when he had played hockey—to strip off his shirt and to rub more dust onto his *banian* beneath it so as to obliterate the pristine whiteness Protima was proud of and in place of shoes to slip into an old pair of rubber-soled *chappals*. A little more dust in his ruffled hair and he had been ready.

"It is observation duty only," he had assured Protima. "We think we are knowing where is some fellow who has stolen one lakh jewellery. That is all."

Best surely not to tell her he was going visiting in Kamatipura.

Nonetheless, as he turned into the familiar lane, mysterious and vibrant now with the evening crowds of labourers from the dense-packed *chawls* of the mill area and the factories further north beginning to swarm in and with its street lamps not yet lit, he found he was rather wishing he had told Protima the true nature of his task. It would have been somehow a little easier, he thought, to act out his pretence of being a customer if he had stated clearly to someone outside of himself that this was what he intended to do.

The solidly fat, venomous *gharwali* was sitting on the top step outside her hut, a *bidi* glowing at her moustached lip. Beside her was a whore. But not Munni. Evidently the old woman had managed to find a replacement for Lakshmi, Lakshmi by now he hoped reunited with the husband who had loved her after he had taken her from Dr. Framrose and put her on a train for Nasik.

But the presence of this other girl created some difficulty for him. He could hardly go up to the *gharwali* pretending to have been attracted by the wares on display and then ask to go with a girl inside he was supposed not to know even existed.

And was Munni going to be inside at all?

Could the *gharwali* have worked out in some fashion that the visitor in her absence the day before who had aided Lakshmi to get away had been there really in order to see Munni? And had she for yet another time had the girl whisked away?

But surely the chances were against that. Munni must be inside the hut, perhaps with a customer already, perhaps not yet painted up enough to come out. But how to get to her?

He walked by, doing no more than glance idly at the pair of them on the top step. But he received in return a teeth-flashing smile from the whore, and ignored it with a show of shamefacedness which was not altogether a show.

Thirty or forty yards further along he turned and began to saunter back. Still no Munni in sight on the steps of the hut, now more easily seen since the lamplighter had reached the nearest lamp. He passed by, meaning this time not even to glance towards the place. But at the last moment he risked a quick flick, in case Munni had just come out.

She had not.

He walked on as far as the entrance to the lane and then turned and went back again, forcing himself to maintain the strolling pace of the scores of other appraising would-be customers beside him.

The new whore was no longer sitting beside the *gharwali*. Instead, glancing round, he saw she had come down into the lane where she was engaged in vigorous talk with a woman who looked like another *gharwali*, no doubt her previous madam. But where was Munni still? Had she had someone with her inside all along? If so the man was being a long time about it, and Kamatipura lane huts were not places for lingering erotic exercises.

He gave the dark open doorway of the hut as lengthy an inspection as he dared. Nothing visible.

"*Hé!* You! You there!"

The *gharwali* was shouting.

She was shouting at him.

There could be no mistake. The crowd round about had thinned and there was no one else within as easy hailing distance.

Had she recognised him? Despite his changed appearance, had she remembered his face?

"You. I have watched you. Looking and looking at my place."

Damn, damn, damn. He had been too obvious.

But the *gharwali* had not finished.

"Why don't you come up? Go in. Good stuff inside. Best only."

He felt a hot blush spread through him, and it was only partly of relief. Mostly it was the hot embarrassment of the teenage boy on his first visit to the area on the point of being trapped into a situation he had wanted to arrive at only in imagination.

"Don't be shy. Don't be shy. Come up. Come up."

He knew the crafty old woman was deliberately shouting more loudly than she needed to with the object of making this hesitating customer go into her hut out of sheer shame.

Well, in doing that she had actually added an extra layer to his disguise.

He kept his smile at this chance success well within himself, and, with a glance to either side under lowered eyes, perhaps a bit too much put on, he hurriedly mounted the steps to the hut.

"Go in, go in, you will find a girl waiting so good you have no notion," the *gharwali* said, grinning round the stub of her acrid-smelling *bidi*. "I have to keep her out of sight, or the whole world would be stamping at my door. So go in, go in and enjoy."

Ghote ducked his head and stepped into the darkness of the shack, its broken door of the day before still askew. Inside the kerosene lantern hanging from a bamboo roof support was giving out a dull orangey light. But by that light, clearly to be seen sitting on the mat on the beaten earth floor, there was little plump Munni.

"Aiee," she said, as he took a step into the circle of the lantern's glow, "I know you from somewhere."

"Ssssh. Ssssh."

Urgently he hushed her.

She at least lowered her voice when she answered. But she was not going to let the subject drop.

"No. No, I have seen. Somewhere, somewhere. But not as customer. It is your face I have seen only, and it is other parts of customers I am seeing most."

She gave a cheerful giggle.

"Yes," Ghote said, in a low whisper. "You have seen me, and not as a customer. You saw me in Falkland Road, in the house you were in there. You saw me on the night—"

"When that man killed poor Kamla," Munni burst in. "Yes, yes. I remember you now. You are a policewalla. Inspector, isn't it?"

"Yes," Ghote said, still urgently whispering. "And I have come here on duty. I very much need to talk with you."

Munni's eyes glinted gleefully in the feeble light of the lantern.

"But you have pretended to be some mill-worker fellow only," she said. "Just so as to see me. Like in the films. *Dishun, dishun.*"

She pointed her plump little fist like a gun and fired off a couple more shots.

"Ssssh," Ghote implored her.

She flashed him a quick grin.

"But you do not want her to know," she said, jerking her chin towards the outside of the hut. "I knew they had pushed me on to her for some reason. I was taken away from Falkland Road to a nice, nice place in Sukhlaji Street, you know, and then suddenly in the middle of the night while I was with a customer only they took me out and brought me here. And I never got my share of the money from that fellow, a double-extra fellow too."

"Yes, yes. All that is so. But the other girl here, will she be coming in at any moment? Where can we go to talk?"

"Beena is okay," Munni answered. "Her *gharwali* has insisted to have her back. But for talk, Inspectorji, there is only one place."

She rose and flicked back one of the hanging lengths of cloth that formed either side of the interior of the little hut. It was a curtain bought long before for the room of some child in a wealthy home that must have made its way down the steps of society by stage after stage until it had reached this hut. It had a design on it of the alphabet in English with pictures. *D is for Dog*, Ghote read. *E is for Elephant.* And behind there was only the broad surface of a bed.

"But—" Ghote said.

"Where else is there, do you think?" Munni whispered. "If you do not want that bitch outside to know we are talking this is the only place."

"All right then."

Munni rolled on to the bed and lay on its far side, plump and pleased.

Ghote moved slowly towards the alphabet curtain.

"No," whispered Munni. "No."

"No what?"

"No, you cannot come in with your clothes on only. Often she comes back in here to see if it is all going well. If she does not find your clothes she will think something is wrong. She is a wicked old woman all the time."

Ghote hesitated, his hand holding back the curtain just where it read *P is for Parrot*. It ought to be for Prostitute, he thought.

From plump and waiting little Munni the stern command came.

"Banian utharo."

With slow, unwilling fingers he peeled the *banian* over his head and let it drop to the floor.

"Pant utharo."

Trousers dropped.

Munni's short skirt and gaudy bra shot out of the cave of the broad bed. Ghote dived in beside her and jerked the alphabet curtain firmly closed.

To his surprise he found, despite the fact that he was stretched out clothesless barely a foot away from a delightful, fresh and stark naked girl that he was in no way aroused.

For a moment he reflected on the oddness of it. How, looked at in one light, a pretty, willing, delicious naked girl could only bring an immediate flare of passion, but yet how the same creature exactly, in exactly the same physical circumstances but viewed in an altogether different light, could seem no more exciting than one of those cold all-white statues of women he had seen in the hall of the Sheriff's house on Malabar Hill.

It was—the sudden comparison popped up in his head—just like that street-seller's toy old D'Sa had shown him with such indignation. One moment showing a naked, flaunting woman, the next just a woman dressed in crude everyday Western clothes. Flick, flack. From one to the other. From the lascivious to the ordinary.

And it was the ordinary girl Munni he was facing at this minute, facing with the object of finding out from her the last detail of what she knew about the man who had been with her friend Kamla shortly before her death.

"Now," he said, "tell me again everything that you saw on the night Kamla was killed.'

Munni lay there in the gloom behind the paper-thin alphabet curtain, still and intent.

"I have thought and thought," she said. "But I did not see anything. The man who came was very early. Before the time business begins. Heerabai had not given us the blessing she gives each night before we start. I was busy with her mustard-oil massage still. Out at the back there in the bathroom you hear nothing of what is happening in the rooms."

That had nagged at Ghote whenever he had considered the detailed circumstances of Kamla's murder.

"Yes," he said. "I have wondered about the sounds. That man beat Kamla very hard. Did none of the girls hear? Did they not speak about it?"

"No, they heard nothing," Munni answered. "I asked them afterwards. But it is noisy always in the street, you know. Girls are shouting at customers and whistling to them. So if Kamla had cried out they would think it was just those sounds only. Or that it was someone playing at being hurt to please a customer. They are sometimes liking us to do that, you know."

"I suppose so," Ghote said, making an effort to keep his voice murmuringly low in case the *gharwali* had taken it into her head to look in.

"Yes, yes," Munni answered with a hint of contempt for such innocence. "That is how you keep a man from really hurting you when you get one who likes to beat you."

"I see. But that night . . . Kamla was beaten very hard then. How would she have let someone do that?"

Munni gave a little sigh in the gloom.

"Well, sometimes-sometimes," she said, "you cannot stop them."

"But that is terrible."

"Yes, it is not nice. But sometimes things are not nice."

For a little Ghote let his mind dwell on the girl's philosophical attitude. The bad and the good, she seemed to take them both as they came. He hoped fervently that nothing irredeemably bad would ever come to her.

"And none of the girls afterwards, when you talked about what had happened, none of them said that they had seen anything of this man? You told me that night they had not. But perhaps afterwards one of them may have remembered something. Did they?"

"No," Munni said. "But, you know, I was taken away from Falkland Road very soon afterwards. So we did not talk much. But I do not think they could have seen or heard anything. They were by that time down at the street door, remember."

"Yes. Yes, I suppose they would not be of any help. But you. You were hurried away from that place. I think it must have been because there is something that you know. Something you know about that very influential man who came that night, a man so influential that Heera was ready to lie and lie about him, to do anything to protect him."

"Oh, but I cannot think what," Munni exclaimed, close to tears.

"What is this? What is this?"

The voice came from just the other side of the thin curtain. The voice of the *gharwali,* sharp and determined.

They lay in petrified silence.

"What is happening there?" came the stern demand again.

"Nothing. Nothing. It is going well," Munni called out.

Then she put her mouth close to Ghote's ear and whispered fiercely.

"Pretend. Pretend. Make the noises. Make them or she will lift the curtain."

Ghote froze.

But for an instant only. Munni was right. If he did not want the *gharwali* to lift the curtain, look at him closely, possibly see who he really was and then call up some *goondas* from outside and tear Munni away from him, he had to act as she had suggested.

Plunging his mind into regions he did not at all wish to go to, he tried to recall what sort of sounds he habitually uttered when he and Protima made love.

Filled to tears-point with a sense of the betrayal he was somehow embarking upon, he produced a quick-breathing series of excited little squeaks and squeals.

"Good, good. More, more," Munni hissed.

He did his best, grimly, to respond.

In a moment he realised that the girl was raising herself up and clambering over him so as to be able to peer out of a corner of the curtain.

Her body was hot against his, lightly sweat-daubed and firm and resilient as new spring growth.

He panted on, bringing out a small cry or two. Were these the sorts of noises on those sex cassettes sold in Hutatma Chowk he had told Inspector D'Sa about? He hoped they were. The *gharwali* would be able to recognise the authentic sounds if anybody could.

"She has gone."

Munni rolled off him, and he lay back as exhausted and empty as if none of what he had been doing had been play-acting.

"Listen," Munni whispered, "I have thought of something."

"Thought of something?"

"Yes. It was because I was thinking that that bitch outside had come in here early."

"Early? You have thought of something about the *gharwali* here?"

"No, no. You idiot. Not her. The man. The man at Falkland Road, who came early."

"Yes? Yes? What is it?"

"He had been there the day before also," Munni whispered. "I had forgotten, but Kamla told me that."

"Just what did she tell?"

"She told me the day before that early that evening she had had a man, one of the rich, rich ones who come in by the back way because they do not want anyone to know they like girls like me and Kamla. He had come early that night, she said, and they had played the whipping game. He had given her rupees fifty and he had said he would come again the next evening, even that he would have to come early again because he would have important, important business later."

It could be the Sheriff, Ghote thought. It could really be. One thing he must do: check on the Sheriff's engagements for the night in question. If he had had some official duty to perform in the first part of that evening, to meet some V.V.I.P. at the airport, to preside at a religious function—there were such functions galore at this time of year—or to be at a film première, then that would clinch it. Almost clinch it.

"Did Kamla tell you anything about this man of the first evening?" he whispered to Munni. "Did she say what he looked like at all?"

"Oh yes, yes. She said when he spoke any words of English it was like a real Englishman, like she had seen in a film once, with a voice like a donkey braying. And she said he was tall and had a very fine body and that he wore white, white shirts always when he came to her so that they looked like a picture of an old ship sailing, like she had on the top of the box she keeps her lipsticks and *kohl* in. And often round his neck he would have a tie like the *pukka* sahib that he was. A tie with stripes. And—and, yes, when he came first, before they began, he would look at her as if he had thought of some joke, with his eyes twinkling and twinkling."

Ghote lay there beside naked little Munni feeling a sense of almost holy awe. There could hardly have been a better description of the Sheriff if it had been a carefully constructed police portrait parlé. His looks, his clothes, his voice even. They had all been whispered to him by this girl just as he had seen them for himself when he had been face to face with the man in his huge house.

Not for the first time in his career he was grateful for the powers of observation to be found in the common man or common woman of Bombay, powers undiluted by the fatal gift of being able to read, of being able to see only in preordained patterns. No, Kamla had seen the Sheriff as he was, and Munni had passed on her words as she had heard them.

He was there. He had, surely, all but that two hundred percent proof. Just check on that evening appointment, and then he could go to the A.C.P. again. This time he would come away having secured the arrest of the man who had strangled two girl prostitutes and would, unless he was put behind bars, go on strangling and strangling.

Yes. Now at last he had his hand on the Sheriff of Bombay.

14

Ghote went to see the A.C.P. first thing next morning. Checking on the Sheriff's engagements had not proved at all difficult. And, yes, on the night of Kamla's murder he had been due at a memorial meeting for Meher Baba, the Parsi great soul, in the Birla Matushri Hall. And he had been there. The *Times of India* for the next day had confirmed it, with a photograph.

Conscious of the weight of the decision the A.C.P. would have to make, Ghote stood rigidly at attention in front of the wide semicircle of his desk and delivered his statement. A statement he had gone over and over in his mind till he was sure of it to the last detail.

The A.C.P. listened in silence. At the beginning his fingers had been playing with one of his initialled metal paperweights. But before long they had ceased all movement.

Outside the large airy cabin, Ghote was distantly aware, crows were cawing and arguing, a dog was barking incessantly and, ever present, there was the rumble and hootings of the traffic. But though he heard them all they never caused his concentration for a moment to waver.

And then he came to the end.

The A.C.P. sat in silence. There was the sound of hurried footsteps clonking by on the wooden veranda on the far side of the closed door.

Then the A.C.P. lifted up the flat brass paperweight he had been playing with at the start of the narrative and held it perhaps an inch above the surface of his desk.

"A prostitute's evidence, Ghote," he said. "The evidence of a prostitute only. Even if you can be sure of finding the wretched girl once again."

"Sir, I am. Sir, I will. I made most careful arrangements with the girl, sir. She is Munni by name. She is very, very much wanting the killer of her friend Kamla to be caught, sir. She has promised by hook or by crook to keep me informed of her each and every whereabouts, sir."

"But nevertheless she remains a person of doubtful reputation. Think of it in court, Inspector. The Defence advocate begins his cross-examination. 'You are named So-and-so?' She states that her name is such. 'And what is your occupation, Shrimati So-and-so?' And she is replying 'I am a prostitute by occupation, sahib.' Laughter in court. Laughter in court, Ghote."

The metal paperweight dropped.

It made a little thump.

"But if she is bringing the truth only . . ."

Ghote's voice faltered. *Speak the truth you are not in court.* The cynical words of the old adage appeared in his mind like a neon advertising sign suddenly switched on.

He thought desperately. And an answer came to him.

"Sir," he said, "there is one witness who saw the Sheriff leaving that place, only just before the body of the girl was discovered. A first-class witness, sir. One that no Defence advocate could challenge."

"Indeed, Inspector? And who is this miracle witness? Not that doctor? Whatshisname? Dr. Framrose? I know about him, Inspector. Doctor he may be, but with the class of patient he has and the work he is doing, sex changes even I am told, you cannot be thinking of calling him."

"No, sir. No, it is not him I would wish to call."

"Then who is it, man?"

"Sir, you yourself gave me his name. It is the Svash—That is, it is Mr. Douglas Kerr, sir, the British film star."

A silence even deeper than before, even colder, descended. The A.C.P. sat unmoving. A lot of time seemed to pass. At last the A.C.P.'s moustache twitched. Once, to the left.

Then he sighed.

"Very well," he said. "Very well, if you think so, Ghote. As a matter of fact, the chap has just come back to Bombay from *shikar* in the Corbett Jungle. I saw it in the *Sunday Observer.* The Gallery column. You say he will definitely be able to state that—that the Sheriff was at this place at that time?"

"No, sir," Ghote admitted. "Not definitely at present. He is not acquainted with the Sheriff, sir. But he saw the person I was seeing there also, the person I am knowing to be the Sheriff. I wish only somehow to show the Sheriff to Mr. Kerr, and then he would confirm, yes or no, whether he saw him at the place in Falkland Road."

"Well, if that is all, Ghote . . . But, mind, when this confrontation takes place you are not to let the Sheriff know its purpose. If the Svashbuckler fails to recognise him, I do not want the Sheriff coming into this cabin and laying down a complaint. Is that understood?"

"Yes, sir. Yes, A.C.P."

"One hundred percent understood?"

"One hundred percent, A.C.P. Sahib."

"No can do, old man. No can do."

Ghote, sitting uneasily late that evening on the edge of a small tweed-covered armchair in the dazzlingly glamorous top-floor bar of the Oberoi-Sheraton Hotel, looked at the Svashbuckler in dismay. He had somehow never thought that his simple request to the former film star to call on the Rajah of Dhar as an admirer of his cricketing skills would be turned down.

But it had been. Flat.

"Please," he said, "why is it no can do?"

The Svashbuckler seemed lost for an answer. He sat staring with heavy sagging cheeks at the scotch whisky Ghote had bought him— How ever much was it going to cost when the bearer brought the bill? —a picture of grumpy unwillingness.

At last he roused himself to give a reply.

"Don't like the idea, old boy. Just don't like it."

"But—but—But I have explained, Mr. Douglas Kerr. I am sorry, Mr. Douglas Carr. We have some reason to believe that the Sheriff may be involved in the event that you were witnessing at that house in Falkland Road. You saw a gentleman leaving those premises. We would be very, very grateful if you would meet the Sheriff and confirm, yes or no, whether he was that gentleman."

"Yes, old boy, you did explain all that. And very confused it sounded."

"But, sir, please, why would you not do this thing?"

"Told you. Don't like it. Don't want to be reminded of that stinking awful place you would insist on taking me to, as a matter of fact."

Ghote thought with a swift dart of bitterness of the Svashbuckler's determination to visit to the full Bombay's notorious Cages and the trouble that had caused him. But he refused to let himself feel aggrieved. The Svashbuckler must be persuaded to play his part in the trapping of the Sheriff and no personal feelings must be allowed to get in the way of doing that. It was the only way of making sure of laying the Sheriff by the heels.

He thought hard.

"Sir, it is a question of justice," he said. "Of acting in the interests of justice."

"I dare say it is, old boy. But I don't feel much like acting in the interests of justice just now, to tell you the truth. I'm afraid your wonderful India is getting me down."

"Oh, I am most sorry to hear. In what manner please is this getting down taking place?"

"Heat. Dirt. Noise. Beggars. Smells. Crowds. Bureaucracy. Incompetence. Incomprehensible English. You name it, laddie."

"Yes. Yes, that is very bad. But all the same, justice must be done, you know."

"But not by me. Not now. Not here. I'm a visitor, old chap. Entitled to some consideration."

The Svashbuckler put his hands on the arms of his chair and began to heave his overlarge body up.

"No, sir," Ghote said. "Please, no. Sir, will you be taking another drink only? A scotch whisky?"

He turned and called, "Bearer! Bearer!"

The Svashbuckler had at least abandoned his attempt to rise. Ghote ordered another whisky and another lime soda.

"Some more nuts also," he added sternly.

"*Ji*, sahib," said the bearer, managing to convey his contempt for such a customer despite the simple acquiescence.

Ghote sat waiting for the drinks and the fresh supply of nuts to arrive. His brain seemed utterly atrophied. What could he say to this man, this bloody Britisher, to persuade him to behave in a proper manner?

The drinks arrived, and the nuts.

And a last recourse as well.

Ghote leant forward to put all the emphasis he could into this final plea of his.

"Mr. Douglas Kerr. You are not simply a British gentleman on holiday in India. You are more. Much, much more. Mr. Douglas Kerr, you are the Svashbuckler. Mr. Douglas Kerr, I have seen you fighting for justice before, many, many times. There was *The Svashbuckler in San Francisco*. Did you not go there at the request of a citizens committee only? And then one by one did you not bump off the five most desperate gangsters terrorising the city?"

"Six, old boy. Six, actually."

"Yes, six. Six. Now I am remembering. And then there was *The Svashbuckler in Sydney*. There you went on the appeal of a girl who was the daughter of your old friend, the policeman who had been wrongly convicted of taking a bribe and had committed suicide. She was begging you to come, and you went. And his name you were clearing when it came to the last reel. That was fighting for justice, Mr. Douglas Kerr."

"Well, yes, old boy, I know. I know."

He seemed to be weakening. Ghote racked his brains furiously for other memories of those teenage cinema-going days.

"And, yes. Yes. There was *The Svashbuckler in Surabaya* also. When your socialite friend was disappearing there, and they were all along saying there was nothing to be done. And then you yourself were investigating and after some time you were unmasking a very terrible white slave racket. Sir, I remember the slogan for that film—*See him secure his lady-love from the slave king*. That was very, very good, Mr. Kerr."

"Yes. Well . . . Well, I suppose I might just give this fellow a tinkle. Ask if I can pop round. One star to another, that sort of thing."

"Oh yes, Mr. Kerr. Please, I am very, very grateful."

"Well, got to do the right thing, you know. Got to do the right thing."

But when down in his suite the Svashbuckler began attempting to do the right thing an unexpected obstacle presented itself. The Bombay telephone system.

The Svashbuckler had asked for a line and dialled. Silence. He had dialled again. A conversation. He had dialled a third time. Silence.

"Bloody Indian phones. They look just like the real thing until you pick one up and try and get a number."

Feeling everything slipping from his grasp again, Ghote suggested taking over. If the Svashbuckler began thinking of all the ills of India once more, would that carefully built-up feeling for justice melt away like morning mists under the fierce blaze of the returning sun?

Ghote dialled. He dialled again. And again. And again. He felt fine prickles of sweat springing up all over the back of his neck despite the coolness of the air-conditioning.

He dialled once again, his sweaty finger slipping in the dial holes. He abandoned that attempt and began once more.

Silence. Pinging reverberant silence.

"Well, dammit," the Svashbuckler said from behind him, "we'll just have to whizz round to his place and beard him in his den. Why not?"

A flush of exuberant optimism erupted in Ghote's mind. Things were going right after all. Things were going to go on going right. They would find the Sheriff at home. The Svashbuckler would make some hearty conversation with him on the subject of cricket. He himself might even bring up the meaning of the elusive word "scourge." Then they would leave with flowery farewells. Out on the gravelly driveway of that huge Malabar Hill house the Svashbuckler would turn to him and say, "That's the chap all right, Inspector." And then he himself would dive for the nearest telephone to ring the A.C.P. There would be a shop with a phone near at hand, and this time there would be no difficulty in getting through. He would utter the words the A.C.P. had told him to use so that no hint of the impending storm would get out before time, those six simple words, *The bird is in the bush.* And then the A.C.P. himself would come round as fast as a car could bring him and he would arrest the Sheriff of Bombay. Yes, arrest him. And it would be all over.

The journey from the Oberoi-Sheraton to Malabar Hill should have been one of the quickest to make in all Bombay, speeding up the wide stretch of Marine Drive now that the evening rush had abated with the dimly seen sea on one side and the bulky blocks of flats lit up on the other. But for once the traffic was not whizzing along at full speed, drivers delighting in the coolness of the air blowing in through open windows. Instead the lines of cars and taxis were proceeding in a series of stop-go jerks. The sound of humming engines was replaced by the irritable hooting of horns.

Ghote began to fret. Were things starting to go badly once again already? Would this Englishman beside him lose patience before long? He might, now that they were at a standstill, open the car door and just stride away. That string of India's defects the fellow had brought out in the top-floor bar of the hotel came back to his mind. What had they been? Heat. Dirt. Noise. Beggars. What else? Yes, incomprehensible English. And often the Svashbuckler had not seemed straightaway to understand what he himself had said.

And now here was a beggar. A grinning boy, jumping out from the darkness with a skimpy piece of dust-blackened cloth in his hand making a show of wiping the car—a police car too, what impudence— and hoping for *baksheesh* from the white sahib he had spotted inside.

Angrily he motioned the imp away.

Then at last the traffic began to move again, and when they reached the Mafatlal Boat Club they saw what had been causing the holdup. A huge painted film hoarding had for some unknown reason fallen from its place by the roadside and had got entangled with a couple of cars. Coolies were still picking up the broken, garish pieces in a desultory fashion and the drivers of the two cars were standing beside their damaged vehicles shouting.

But at last they themselves were clear, and the Sheriff's house only a few hundred yards away. Ghote began in his mind rehearsing the words he hoped the Svashbuckler would say, words of extravagant praise for the Sheriff as a cricketer.

Then, just as they were slowing to a halt in front of the house, something, some chance or instinct, made him look up and he saw by the light of a street lamp some way further along the road a familiar, tall, suited figure in the act of disappearing into a yellow-topped taxi.

The Sheriff. The Sheriff himself. And, thanks to that absurd delay in Marine Drive, they had missed him by less than two minutes.

He cursed.

But then a thought struck him. Why should the Sheriff, the still very wealthy Rajah of Dhar who must own three or four cars, be getting into a humble anonymous taxi almost on his own doorstep? The answer came to him in the same breath as the query. The man was going in secret to visit Kamatipura.

To visit Kamatipura. The black urge had come upon him again.

By his side the Svashbuckler was already heaving his bulk out of the car. Ghote seized him unceremoniously by the arm and tugged him back in.

"That taxi," he shouted to his driver. "The one that has just left under that lamp there. Follow it. Don't let it out of your sight."

They started away in a fine slew of speed. But there was in fact no difficulty in following the taxi as it made its way, to Ghote's mingled fear and justification, to Kamatipura.

But when they reached Falkland Road and were butting their way slowly through the evening throng of the brothels' customers the taxi ahead made no attempt to stop. The familiar red-painted sign outside Dr. Framrose's dispensary, *Sex Diseases, Sex Changes,* slid by and was lost.

It did, however, remind Ghote once again of that nagging question the excitable Parsi had put into his head, the meaning of the word "scourge." It was, surely, something that you used to clean things with, to clean them altogether thoroughly. Something that you used to clean things by rubbing them with something rough, or with a harsh flow of water. Or was that "scour"? Was there an English word "scour" also?

Perhaps this after all would be a possible moment to deal at least with this worry. After all, the Svashbuckler was an Englishman. He would be more likely to know even than the Sheriff.

"Mr. Douglas Kerr, sir," he began after a preliminary cough. "There is something perhaps you would be able to tell, a thing that has been somewhat bothering and upsetting me."

"Oh yes, old boy?"

The Svashbuckler did not sound very interested. But no matter.

"It is just this only, Mr. Douglas Kerr. Some days past I was having conversation with a gentleman, conversation in English, and he was using a certain word. It is a word I am finding I do not know exactly what it is meaning."

"Oh yes?"

Really the fellow was hardly listening.

He took a deep breath none the less and plunged in.

"Yes, Mr. Douglas Kerr. It is this word. Scourge. Scourge. Are you please able to tell me its exact meaning?"

"What was that, old boy?"

The yellow roof of the taxi ahead was easy to follow. It was the only vehicle brave enough to push through the milling brothel customers all over the roadway. But the Svashbuckler seemed to be concentrating on it with tremendous keenness.

The way he was leaning forward, peering ahead, made Ghote recall from the far past the car chase in *The Swashbuckler in Surabaya*. But there the background had been winding roads through lush jungle and the vehicles involved had been going at a crazy speed, clouds of dust rising behind them.

But there was only the bright light of the street lamps and the areas of darkness between them, the girls in the Cages at the windows above looking down and calling out and the men reluctantly making way for their vehicle. So what was the fellow play-acting like this for?

"Scourge, Mr. Douglas Kerr?" he repeated more loudly. "Scourge? What is the meaning of this word?"

"Oh well. It means a whip, I suppose, old chap. Yes, some sort of a whip, far as I know."

A whip. Ghote felt himself going alternately hot and cold. A whip, and he had been going to ask the Sheriff himself the meaning of the word. Why, it would have been the next thing to putting a direct accusation of whip murder to him. It would have alerted him completely to what was suspected about him. The fellow would only had to have heard this seemingly clever beginning to an interrogation to take fright and flee. He could easily get on to a plane and leave the country, go somewhere where he could not be extradited and where he could indulge his bestial propensities to the full.

And the A.C.P., what would he have said if he had heard this direct order not to alert the Sheriff in any way had been so flagrantly disobeyed? What would he have done?

He felt the sweat wetting the whole back of his trousers as he sat on the scuffed leather car seat.

Then the taxi ahead jockeyed its way out of Falkland Road and entered Vallabhbhai Patel Road, V.P. Road. Where on earth was it making for?

In little more than another minute that question was answered. The taxi came to a halt.

Ghote recognised at once where they had come to. The tall building outside which the Sheriff's taxi had stopped was hung from top to bottom with long strings of coloured lights, a bright invitation in the velvety darkness of the night. It was Pavan Pool, that curious group of dwellings set round an inner compound that was the traditional home of Bombay's courtesans, some five thousand souls in all counting in the musicians who played for the women and the male hangers-on who lived idle lives at their expense.

So had the Sheriff changed his hunting ground? Was he looking for prey among a different sort of women from the plain whores of Falkland Road, Kamatipura and Sukhlaji Street? The courtesans, though ready to form liaisons with men either for the length of a night or in a more permanent way, were before anything else singers and dancers, entertainers deriving from the legendary courtesans of places like Lucknow in the north, the easers of the hard hours of Moghul princes.

True, not many of them now practised the delicate arts of their grandmothers and great-grandmothers, the arts Dr. Framrose had been speaking of when he had quoted from some ancient book on the duties of a courtesan mother. Instead, from what he had heard from such visitors to the place as Sub-Inspector D'Silva, who claimed to know its every corner, they mostly imitated the easy rhythms and half-Westernised ways of the *filmi* world. But none the less they were a group apart, living a crowded, often sordid but yet vital life within the confines of this enclave, Pavan Pool.

This world into which the tall figure of the Sheriff was at this moment entering, walking carelessly through the wide open tall iron-work gates painted an alluringly soft gold.

"Hey. Yes."

It was the Svashbuckler, sitting beside him where they had come to a halt some fifteen yards distant from the gates and peering out into the exciting night.

"Yes? Yes, what?"

"It's him. The chappie I saw at that place. He's the cricketer fellow. The whatsit. The jolly old Sheriff of Bombay."

15

Ghote was tempted to jump out of the car, find a telephone and ring the A.C.P. there and then. But he thought of what he feared that the Sheriff had come to Pavan Pool to do. To entice away a different sort of girl it now seemed, to take her somewhere where he could beat her and then strangle her to death with the whip he had used. It would not be easy, in fact, for him to leave with any of the courtesans till the evening's performances were over but nevertheless it would be no more than a sensible precaution to follow the man in and to see just what he was doing.

Then what if the Svashbuckler, for all the decisive way he had just identified the Sheriff, had made a mistake? It was vital to have every stage in the process of recognition carried out with the maximum formality circumstances permitted. With any luck the Svashbuckler would never have to appear to give evidence in court since surely the Sheriff with such a strong case against him now would not, as the A.C.P. had forecast of him, contest the matter every inch of the way. But to have the Svashbuckler and the Sheriff meet face to face in front of witnesses, that would be worth any amount of trouble to achieve.

He explained as much of this as he felt necessary to his companion.

"Then off we go, old chap," the Svashbuckler said. "And anyhow, if half what you tell me is true, I'd like to see inside this place."

They left the car, advanced along the street towards the strings of dangling coloured lights and went through the gates that would be firmly closed at the establishment's curfew hour when all visitors had to leave. And not a few would go with one or another of the courtesans beside them.

A short archway lit only by the light of a *paan* stall against its wall and they were in the wide compound formed by three tall buildings, their ornate old carved wooden pillars and arches visible here and there in the light coming from the balconies above the ground-level barred window apertures with their tantalising glimpses of life going on inside. They made their way past groups of idle young men, mostly notably well dressed in fine cotton shirts or silk *kurtas* with hair tumbling down in glisteningly oiled locks, sitting or squatting playing cards or gambling with dice. In one corner under the hard glare of a petromax lamp a group of players was clustered round the square white surface of a *carom* board watching the round pieces being skilfully tapped across its chalk-dusted surface. A spasm of argument broke out among them and a knife was half-drawn.

"I say, old man, you don't think . . ." the Svashbuckler began, and then fell silent.

Across on the far side Ghote caught his looked-for glimpse of a tall, white-suited figure.

He hurried after him as he disappeared into one of the dark doorways, the Svashbuckler close at his shoulder, stumbling over the occasional heap of rubbish on the ground.

At the doorway they were in time to see their quarry ascending ancient wooden stairs painted a bright if dirtied shade of pink. They set off into ever-gathering darkness in his wake. Two floors up, feeling their way now as much as seeing it and trying hard to distinguish the Sheriff's heavy-shoed steps from the flap of other visitors' *chappals,* Ghote realized that the Sheriff had stopped climbing and had gone off along one of the tall corridors opening out from each landing.

They found it a little better lit when they reached the stair head in their turn and they were able to stop and keep the tall, white-suited figure under observation with more confidence.

The Sheriff seemed very much at ease. At the doorway of almost every one of the little rooms clustered along the corridor like the cells of a honeycomb he stopped, looked in for a moment and then passed on. Once he stood staring for as much as three minutes and only when he broke off did Ghote, the Svashbuckler still almost brushing against him, set off in pursuit again, glancing in like his quarry at the open doorways.

"Bit garish, the rooms, aren't they?" the Svashbuckler ventured to murmur after a little.

It was true that they were not particularly good advertisements for the supposedly refined culture of Pavan Pool. Their walls were brightly tiled in colours reminiscent to Ghote of the hall in the Sukhlaji Street brothel and the carpets that covered their floors for the benefit of the dancing girls, though thick, were extremely vivid in colour. Most of them had framed coloured photographs hanging in jostling profusion and two had television sets perched on shelves in the corner while a third boasted a brightly illuminated tank of darting little fish. The girls in the rooms, mostly still sitting against the walls waiting to begin their performances, were dressed in saris of the gaudiest sort and were chattering and laughing in the loudest of voices or busy tying on their anklet bells amid a continuous soft jingling.

In one of the rooms a girl was already dancing to music that was undisguisedly *filmi*. Her hips, wriggling as she turned, looked to Ghote's mind more like a giant pair of boxing gloves than anything else. The whole dance, indeed, was more acrobatic than elegant and as they left they saw the dancer fling herself backwards and drop down on to knees and extended hands, much naked stomach on display, and advance beat by beat towards an appreciative leering row of spectators. Fingers went to mouths and shrill whistlings sounded out. High-denomination notes were thrust forward with many a grunted "Wah, wah," then rapidly collected and piled in triumph on top of the room's harmonium.

When, however, they reached the doorway at which the Sheriff had lingered—he was now almost at the end of the corridor, once again stopping to watch for more than a quick glimpse—things were different.

Here, Ghote realised at once, was no crude imitation of the gaudy goings-on of the *filmi* world. A girl in a brilliant blue sari, her ears hung with heavy, cascading silver earrings, was dancing to the music of a squatting bespectacled harmonium player with a gracefulness that set up in him an immediate response. Yes, he thought, in the days of the Moghuls it must have been something like this. His mind went back to the appalling Mujra Nite at Colaba when he had gone to hunt up Sub-Inspector D'Silva. How different was that blatant display of sexuality from this girl, dancing it seemed almost for herself, for the dance's sake.

"This is more like it," the Svashbuckler murmured in his ear. "But I wonder what your Sheriff chappie has found that made him move on from here?"

His words brought Ghote sharply back to the reasons for his presence at Pavan Pool. He must first make sure the Sheriff was not immediately seeking prey, and then he must get the Svashbuckler and the Sheriff to meet face to face.

That should not, he thought, be too difficult once the Sheriff has settled down in one of the rooms or another as seemed now to be his intention. He himself could then make out with reason that he was escorting this V.V.I.P. to one of the sights of Bombay where a police officer was likely to be helpful. He could pretend to recognise the Sheriff, thank him on Ved's behalf for that message scrawled on the photograph—that message and the fingerprints that were all round it —and after that he could naturally introduce one distinguished person to another. And there would be plenty of witnesses to the meeting.

"Yes, we will go," he said.

It did not take them long to locate the Sheriff. He had settled quietly in almost the last of the rooms, and was sitting cross-legged and shoeless on a mattress that ran all along the wall nearest its door, his back resting against a cushion covered in a clean white pillowcase even though the blue paint of the wall behind was scabbed and peeling.

So no question yet, Ghote thought, of any attempt to lure away anyone for his obscene purposes. Indeed, the fellow looked very much as if he was there for the rest of the evening. Perhaps the sort of girl here did not set up in him the black desire that had brought about the deaths of Kamla and Sweetie. And possibly of others.

A girl was dancing as a woman sang, and Ghote realised again that here were performances of an altogether higher class, better even than that of the dancer who had given him for a few moments the feeling of being a nawab of old watching in silken-cushioned ease a dance directed at himself alone.

The dancer here, a creature of startlingly refined beauty wearing a skirt with heavy embroidery at the hem over thigh-clinging *churidar*, gave him that feeling certainly but even more strongly. And the singer, a maturely plump woman in a gauzy black sari, sitting on the floor with her legs to one side and using elegant hands to caress and shape the phrases of her song, was again a figure seemingly from a more dignified, more leisurely age.

There was only one other spectator, a bulbously fat man with a bald head over which two or three strands of oiled hair were carefully stretched. He was tucked into the far corner of the long mattress, leaning on two separate pillows. His eyes were gently glowing with delight and his plump fingers were marking out the shape of the music almost as if they were moulding some delicious sweetmeat before popping it into his rosebud mouth.

Ghote removed his shoes, slipped into the room and sat. The Svashbuckler followed suit, lowering himself with a puffy grunt onto the mattress, his long legs awkwardly stuck out. Ghote glanced at the Sheriff, but he was so absorbed in the music that he had taken no notice at all.

Well, there would be time enough.

In a short while a flower vendor came in, his arm hung with a bee-swarm mass of flowers, garland after garland of creamy-white, star-shaped tuberoses. Their fine sweet scent entered with him, suddenly submerging the grosser odours of the room, perfume, hair oil, sweat. Silently and unobtrusively the man went to each of the women, handing them garlands for their hair—the dancer hardly stopped to implant hers dextrously on the back of her head—and then giving others to the onlookers, stooping to slip them onto extended wrists.

"God," murmured the Svashbuckler.

But he sniffed contentedly at the little white flowers when they were in place.

The music was being played by three musicians, one with a sitar, a drummer on the *tabla* and a humbler provider of droning rhythm in the background. The sounds they were producing swam languorously, quickened into sharp rapidity, sank back again. The high-pitched voice of the singer soared with or caressed each word of her song with every ounce of meaning that could be got into it, each mention of the beautiful soon-to-die rose, of the moon, of the loved one distant but remembered.

> Who snatched at my veil in the crowded bazaar?
> This moonlight night he is late in coming.

Ghote, who had not often heard singing of this quality, was rapidly lost in it. And lost, too, in the skirt-lifting swirl of the young dancer, her whole body echoing the music as the drummer heightened his rhythm to an electric burst of sound. He felt as if he was being made love to, himself alone. And he was sure that the pot-bellied man in the corner felt just the same, as surely did the Sheriff, sitting entranced, his head very slightly moving to the music's beat.

How extraordinary this is, Ghote thought. It is sex as blatantly extended as it is by the girls who lean against the thin bars of the Cages and hiss at passers-by. But, though the sex is there, the exchange between female and male, this is something that arouses the baser instincts not at all. Not even, he was certain, those in the Sheriff, for all the fears he had earlier had about him.

> Night after night I have waited.
> The lamps are fading.

And the sad, caressing voice died away as the song came to its end. The Sheriff looked up from his trance and stared round with a vague air much in contrast with the teasing authority that he had always shown before.

Ghote swallowed.

This was the moment.

He leant forward on the mattress.

"It is Sheriff Sahib," he said. "We were meeting the other day only. I am Inspector Ghote. You were doing me the very, very great favour to accept to open the Police Vegetable and Flower Show. You were also signing your photo for my son, Ved, and writing a message. He is very, very grateful. And this"—his voice suddenly went dry on him—"and this is a very, very distinguished visitor from the U.K. He is the very, very famous film star, known by the name of the Svashbuckler. It is Mr. Douglas Kerr, only you are pronouncing it Carr."

The Sheriff's eyes lit up.

"The Swashbuckler," he said. "My dear chap. Why, I got six of the best once for cutting prep at the Doon School just to watch you. *The Swashbuckler in Sydney*, *The Swashbuckler in Surabaya*, *The Swashbuckler in Singapore*. I've seen them all."

"*The Swashbuckler in San Francisco?*" the purple-nosed, sagging-cheeked Englishman asked.

"Certainly, certainly, my dear fellow. And the Indian films, too. Not very like the India I knew, but jolly good all the same. *The Swashbuckler Meets the Evil Kali* and *The Swashbuckler Meets the Evil Kali Again*. Marvellous."

The two of them shook hands enthusiastically.

"Oh yes," said the Sheriff, "and may I introduce Mr. Jesingbhai Patel, a fellow lover of this ancient art whom I bump into here from time to time?"

The man in the corner, who had been listening with rabid attention to the conversation, greeted the Svashbuckler with folded hands and an inclination of his pot-bellied waist.

This is too good to be true, Ghote thought. Here is a person, probably a respected Gujarati businessman, whose actual name I have been given and who has witnessed the meeting between the Sheriff and the Svashbuckler. All is well. Well. Well.

The sitar player, cross-legged with his instrument, had begun to sound out the tentative beginning of a new song. Mr. Patel wriggled his plump shoulders happily into the pillows at his back. The Sheriff's attention turned to the dancing girl as she got to her feet again.

Ghote leant closer to the Svashbuckler and spoke quietly.

"You are confirming that this is the man you were seeing?"

The Svashbuckler turned towards him. His pouched eyes bore an expression of distress.

"Well . . ." he said. "But, old boy, the fellow's such a nice chap. I really don't . . ."

No, Ghote yelled within himself. No, you are not going to go back on it now.

"Mr. Douglas Kerr," he whispered furiously, "is that the man? Yes or no? Yes or no, please."

The Svashbuckler uttered a little groan.

"Yes," he said. "Yes, it's the chappie all right."

"Very good," Ghote murmured. "Now, listen please. I have to go make a very, very urgent telephone call. You will stay here. You have the music to listen to, that dancer to watch. Nothing could be more nice. But in the unlikely event of the Sheriff beginning to go, you are to go with him. Yes? Then as soon as you can you should telephone in your turn to let me know where you both are. Here is my card. See it has the number on it."

The Svashbuckler looked no happier. But he took Ghote's card and pushed it into his pocket.

Ghote got to his feet. The singer was in full flow now, and he felt a pang at leaving. But duty called.

He slipped out of the room, got into his shoes, made his way along the corridor, down the dark well of the pink-painted staircase and out into the compound.

Hurrying across its ill-lit space, he cursed himself for not having spent a few minutes locating a telephone before he had entered Pavan Pool. Now that he had secured beyond doubt that vital agreement from the Svashbuckler, he felt, irrational though he knew it to be, that every second somehow counted. If the A.C.P. could not come to take the Sheriff into custody straight away, he had a deep foreboding that somehow something would happen to let that invincible figure escape even at this last hour.

He shook his head angrily.

Dammit, this was a matter of logic. Of simple logic. A girl had been murdered, brutally murdered, and shortly afterwards a man had been seen, by himself and by the guaranteed witness the Svashbuckler, leaving the place where the murder had been committed. Then he himself had taken the weapon with which the killing had been done, that whip hanging there in the room, and had delivered it, however improperly according to the rules of evidence, to the experts in the Fingerprint Bureau, who had found with scientific certainty a clear set of prints on its handle. Next, he had obtained a good set of the Sheriff's prints on an excellent surface for such evidence, namely a glossy photograph, which the Sheriff had additionally signed with his own clear signature—plus a message about keeping a straight bat—and the Fingerprint Bureau had had no difficulty in confirming that the prints on the whip and the prints on the photograph were one and the same.

So it was clear, clear as could be, that the Sheriff of Bombay had murdered the prostitute Kamla in the house in Falkland Road, and from the similarity of the modus operandi it was almost as certain that he had murdered the call-girl student Veena Bhaskar, known as Sweetie.

It was logic. All simple, plain logic. Why then this fear that something was going to go astray even now? No reason. No reason at all. Oh yes, the Sheriff might take it into his head to leave Pavan Pool before the A.C.P. could reach there, and the Svashbuckler might not succeed in staying with him. But that would only be a temporary setback. The Sheriff of Bombay was a person there would be no difficulty in quickly finding once it was known that he was wanted.

So everything was as right as it could be.

Passing at the gate the *chowkidar,* smart in his police-like forage cap and well-polished Sam Browne belt, he found nevertheless that he was possessed by the idea that he must get to a phone without the least delay.

He looked up and down the length of V.P. Road. There were shops there, to left and right, with lights still shining from their narrow interiors. Which was most likely to have a phone? Ah, there, judging by the sign over the door saying *Rice Plate Ready Trust in God* was an Irani restaurant. That surely was the best bet.

He hurried over and entered.

The proprietor, pasty-faced and weary-looking after a long day, was leaning against his counter underneath a hanging wire basket containing three sad-looking boiled eggs.

"Telephone?" Ghote barked out.

The man hardly bothered to look up.

"Not working," he said.

Ghote felt all his forebodings were coming true. He drew in a deep breath. Just because one phone was out of order, it did not mean that he would fail to get through to the A.C.P. altogether, or that the A.C.P. would not get to Pavan Pool within half an hour.

"Where is there another telephone somewhere near?" he asked.

The Irani shrugged.

"Go along a little way," he said. "You will surely find a *paanwalla* with one."

Ghote marched out and banged on down the street. There seemed not to be a *paan* stall open anywhere.

A.C.P. Sahib, A.C.P. Sahib, he found he was muttering, do not be out of touch now. Do not be out of touch. Do not be out of touch.

At the next corner there was another Irani restaurant. He almost ran up to it. Its door was still wide open. Three customers were sitting at one of its tin tables over tiny cups of "single" tea passing the time. Above them there hung a fly-spotted notice saying *Do Not Sit Idle Between 1 and 2.* But the busy lunch hour was far past.

He drew in a deep breath. If I ask with politeness, he promised himself, there will be a phone and it will be working.

"Excuse please," he said to the owner, almost the pasty replica of the man he had spoken to before, "do you have telephone?"

"Oh yes, sahib."

"It is working?"

"If God wills it."

The man pushed the instrument towards him. He lifted the receiver and dialled, forcing himself to do so steadily.

The A.C.P.'s phone was answered promptly.

"Is A.C.P. Sahib there please? It is Inspector Ghote."

"Ah, Inspector Ghote," the servant who had answered said. "A.C.P. Sahib is saying I must take message if you are ringing and he would come as soon as he can. Yes, please?"

"Yes," Ghote said, with a new access of foreboding at the absence of the A.C.P. "This is the message. *The bird is in the bush.* Do you understand that? *The bird is in the bush.*"

"*Ji,* sahib. The bird—" For a fearful moment the man hesitated "Is in the bush."

"Good. Good. First class. Pass it on at once. At once. The bird is in the bush and Inspector Ghote is at Pavan Pool. I will wait at the gate. Do you understand?"

"*Ji,* sahib. Pavan Pool. At the gate. The bird is in the bush also."

Ghote rang off.

Surely everything would be all right now, despite the failure to contact the A.C.P. directly.

He paid the Irani and left the restaurant, weaving his way through the evening strollers, trying to persuade himself there was now no great need to hurry.

A beggar boy came towards him, a tiny, bulging-stomached figure in dirty khaki shorts and equally dirty torn shirt. He could not have been more than six, and was holding out in front of himself a small tray on which there were some glinting objects which he was vaguely thrusting towards any passer-by who caught his attention as if he only half-remembered what it was that he had been told to do.

Ghote was one of his victims. He looked down at the boy's tray with the four or five objects it held. Then he looked again. The boy was hawking just the same sort of little pictures that Inspector D'Sa had been so enraged by when he had met him on his way to see the A.C.P. and receive those instructions to take the Svashbuckler on the tour of the Cages which had been the start of this whole overwhelming affair. No doubt a consignment of the wretched toys had become available cheap and someone who employed beggar boys had unloaded the things onto a whole tribe of them.

They reminded him of how he had felt when he had been lying next to little Munni and had obtained the information that had led him onwards when he had feared all was hopeless. He had remembered then the curious effect of flick-flack. Clothes: no clothes. Munni an object of desire: Munni a source of information purely.

"How much?" he asked the tiny fellow in front of him.

"Twenty paisa, sahib. Twenty only."

Ghote dropped a coin on the boy's tray, a round silvery fifty-paisa piece. The boy ought to have stated a higher price and bargained his way down. But he was plainly too young to remember to do it.

Ghote slipped the awful little toy into his pocket without pausing to flick the clothed woman into a naked one.

He thought of what he would have to do during the next half hour, or longer if the A.C.P. was hard to get hold of. No doubt the Sheriff would still be where he had left him. Performances such as the one he was watching went on till the Pavan Pool curfew hour. So it would probably be best to join him for a few minutes until the earliest time the A.C.P. was likely to arrive at the gate. That would plainly be the most sensible course. To check on his quarry. But taking it he knew he would feel he was somehow betraying the man whose delight in that music and that dance he had shared.

And then he found, just as he passed the *paan* stall in the Pavan Pool archway, that there had come into his head a monstrous thought. An impossible thought.

What if, after all, the Sheriff was not guilty of that murder in the house in Falkland Road? What if that train of logic that had seemed so well linked as he had left to find a telephone had a flaw in it?

He could bring none to mind. But now his thoughts were in a whirl of confusion. He longed to be at his desk at Headquarters, with a sheet of paper in front of him, where he could consider in quiet, write down every fact step by step. See what in the end they came to beyond doubt. Where, if anywhere, that logical flaw lay.

But at this moment he could think of nothing but that there was, there might be, some false link in the chain of reasoning that had only a few minutes earlier seemed so strong.

He found he was crossing the dark compound at breakneck speed, heading towards the doorway he had taken before as if every second counted.

He had been forbidden by the A.C.P. to ask the Sheriff any questions that would alert him. He had been forbidden in the strongest terms.

He was going to disobey.

16

Ghote found the Sheriff with the Svashbuckler and fat Mr. Patel almost exactly as he had left them, except that the Svashbuckler had managed to heave his long legs round beside him on to the white mattress. The singer was in full voice as Ghote slid down himself, picked up the garland he had dropped from his wrist and sniffed at it again. Its odour was strong as ever.

But the music that had wafted him away earlier seemed to have lost all its former power.

He found he had no room in his head now for the fading rose, the full moon, the departing lover, however rich was the emotion with which they were being summoned up. He could think of one thing only. That he was going to defy the A.C.P.'s order and put a direct question to the Sheriff that should, one way or the other, establish him as the man guilty of the Falkland Road murder. Or lift that shadow from him, unlikely though that seemed.

But unless he made his move within the next few minutes the A.C.P. might arrive and, on the strength of the evidence he himself had put together, carry out the arrest. Perhaps the arrest of an inno- cent man, and a man of as much influence as any in all the heights of Bombay society.

Yet that doubt had arisen in his mind, however little logical sub- stance there seemed to be for it, and he dared not rest until he had put it to the trial. Ghost-like it might be. But it stood there, solid as a stark black stone.

> Until I have darkened my eyes with *kohl*,
> Until I have adorned my hair,
> You must wait.

Would the song never end? What nonsense words like that were. Dream stuff.

Then, quite suddenly it seemed, the song was over. The notes of the sitar died away. The drummer's fingers dropped from his stretched skins. Mr. Patel and the Sheriff held out rupee notes by the fistful to the singer.

Ghote pushed himself up, moved along to where the Sheriff sat cross-legged, bent low and addressed him.

"Sheriff Sahib, there is a very important matter. I am wishing to speak with you in secret and confidence. Would you kindly come just outside?"

The Sheriff's eyebrows mounted slightly in his handsome face. The old teasing personage was back. The rapt listener to the music from the fabled past had drained away in an instant.

"Secret and confidence, Inspector? What can this be? Are you going to arrest me under the Immorality Act, if there is such a thing?"

"Sir, it is most urgent," Ghote answered, taking no pains to keep down-to-earth stubbornness out of his voice.

The Sheriff sighed.

"Oh, very well, Inspector, if you say so. Never let it be thought that the Sheriff of Bombay shirked any one of the calls made upon him."

He rose easily to his feet, glanced down at the Svashbuckler busy massaging his thighs, murmured an apology to him and preceded Ghote out into the dimly lit corridor.

"Will this do, Inspector? Or do you want to take me down to that evil-smelling compound there?"

"No, Sheriff Sahib, this will be very fine. I may have one question to put to you only."

"A question? What a policeman you are, Inspector."

The corridor was deserted. From the rooms to either side music was coming, the voice of a girl singing a song from some film or other and the soft, insistent tinkle of anklet bells with the beat of naked feet as a pair of dancers danced.

"Well, Inspector?"

Ghote felt he could see those eyebrows gently raising up again, though in the gloom he could barely make out the Sheriff's face.

It is now or never, he thought. Now I will know.

He gulped in a breath.

"Sheriff Sahib," he said, "that night in the house in Falkland Road when the *gharwali* Heera hurried you outside, what had you done?"

It was asked. The fatal question.

The Sheriff appeared quite unmoved. But there was a long tingling silence between them.

The brash music from the rooms behind sounded on.

"Well . . ." the Sheriff said at last. "How did you come to know that I was there, Inspector?"

"I myself was there also. I saw you as I entered that place."

"You did? I thought I'd got away in time."

"What in time, Sheriff Sahib? After what had happened there?"

Again there was a long pause. The music went on, garish and loud.

"Well, I suppose I know what you must be thinking. There'd been a murder there, and you believe I was responsible."

"And were you?" Ghote asked. "Was it you who killed that girl there?"

A tiny pause now. Barely two beats of the insistent music.

"No. No, Inspector, it was not me."

Ghote waited. He sensed that, left to himself, the Sheriff would be unable to resist adding something to that flat, level denial. Something that perhaps would, in some detail or other, come eventually to contradict it.

And before long the Sheriff did speak again.

"But I can see, Inspector, that you are hardly going to feel that my merely stating that I was not responsible is enough. After all, as you yourself saw, I did beat a very hasty retreat that evening. I suppose that alone makes me look guilty. But I am not. I really am not. Yet how am I going to convince you of the fact?"

He sighed.

"I suppose it will hardly be enough if I tell you that I left the place almost as soon as I had arrived. I used to go in always round by the back, you know. Not a very salubrious way, but one doesn't quite like to be seen entering a place like that, and a lot of the people out in Falkland Road would know my face. The penalty of playing cricket rather too well."

Again he came to a stop. And again Ghote waited.

After a little the dribble of words resumed once more.

"Yes, I had only just arrived, though of course I can't prove that, unless you're going to believe the dreadful Heera. One takes precautions not to be with anyone one knows on those occasions, using a taxi instead of any of the cars and so on, as I do even coming here. And so there's no one reliable to say where I was at what particular time. You'll just have to take my word for it, Inspector. Not that there's any special reason why you should. But there it is. I arrived, a little later than sometimes and almost straight away that fat old monster of a *gharwali* came padding along all smelling of mustard oil and told me that she had just heard that a police party was on its way. Come to show some visitor or other round, the way they like, you know. And she said I had better get out quickly. It was only the next day, when I went back hoping to keep the date I hadn't managed to the evening before, that I learnt there had been a murder there and that poor Kamla was the victim."

Again he ceased speaking. But this time Ghote guessed that a sharp prod might be more effective than repeated silence.

"Kamla?" he said. "You knew the name."

The Sheriff did not reply. A man came staggering out from the last of the rooms along the corridor, plainly drunk. He turned towards them, a big fellow. A Sikh. For a moment he looked at them, as if he was going to challenge their right to be there. But then he blundered past and lurched his way towards the staircase.

The Sheriff gave a long sigh.

"Oh yes, Inspector," he said, "I knew Kamla. I knew her very well. And that, in a way, is why I've kept quiet about the whole business. If it hadn't been Kamla in particular who had been killed, and killed in the way I gather she was, and if as well I had known that you had spotted me there, I might have tried having a discreet word with the Commissioner or somebody so as to avoid any misunderstanding."

This time Ghote thought that silence was again his best weapon. And so it proved. Almost at once the Sheriff went on once more.

"But I left it too late, didn't I? You saw me fleeing the scene of the crime and now you've caught up with me, though I wonder why you've been quite so long about it. I mean, when you came to see me— Ah. Ah, yes. I understand now. That photograph I signed for you. Fingerprints. That was very clever of you, Inspector. Very skilful."

"It—It was truly my son's photo that I was bringing," Ghote felt constrained to say. "I was not cheating altogether."

There had been something in the Sheriff's tone that had made him want to have nothing that was false between them. The way he had said that the photograph trick had been skilful had not been a snarl of acknowledged defeat. It had been rather a small compliment in passing, genuinely paid.

But there was something more to come. And it would be not merely details fleshing out an already admitted fact. So it was important that all that was said by either of them should be steadfastly true.

"Well," the Sheriff answered, "I'm glad to know that, Inspector. So has your—What was the boy's name? Ah, yes. Ved. Has your Ved seen my message to him? Keep a straight bat, eh? You must have thought that was pretty hypocritical of me."

"No," Ghote said, truth-telling still. "Ved has not seen the photo. It may be necessary to hold it as evidence."

"Yes, of course. Stupid of me."

The Sheriff moved uneasily in the dim light. From the rooms along the corridor the sound of music rose and fell.

"Well, Inspector," the Sheriff resumed, "I think the moment has come for me to play my straight bat. Been putting it off rather. Hoping that it wouldn't be necessary. But I see now that it is. You found my fingerprints in Kamla's room, didn't you?"

Now Ghote thought he must after all use half a lie.

"Yes," he said.

He recalled the whip with the Sheriff's prints on it and concealing it to circumvent Sub-Inspector D'Silva, the too easily bribed.

"Yes," the Sheriff echoed. "My fingerprints in Kamla's room. You must think you've got a pretty good case. But—but, well, the fact is that I didn't kill the poor girl. And now, I see, I'll have to try to tell you why there never could be any question of my doing such a thing."

Then, for the first time, Ghote began to feel that the unaccountable doubt which had risen up in his mind to sit in it like a black impenetrable stone might after all prove to be a true sign.

"Go on, Sheriff Sahib," he said.

"Yes."

The Sheriff could be seen in the half-dark squaring those shoulders he had squared to face fast bowling so many times in the past.

"Yes, well, this is the reason, Inspector. You see, I used to go to poor Kamla for one very special purpose."

He gave an abrupt bark of a laugh. But when he resumed he appeared to have veered away once more from the revelation he had been on the point of making.

"I daresay you've heard the tales they tell about me," he said. "I dare say they're even part of the case you've built up against me in your mind. The Don Juan touch. Our modern Krishna. I heard someone say that of me the other day. And I must admit I play up to that sort of talk. It amuses me. I'm even not above dropping in the odd reference to my notorious grandfather, the one who burnt the polo pony you know. Yes, I've played up to all that, and serves me right now. Serves me right."

"Not a modern Krishna?" Ghote said, feeling he had inserted a thin blade into a fine crack and was with infinite caution beginning to lever up—something.

Something, he knew not what.

"No. No Krishna. There haven't really been all that many *gopis* actually. Oh yes, I've taken girls out. Kissed them, cuddled them. But in India, anyway, it isn't kiss and tell, as you know. It's rather more get kissed and hint. Hint at a whole lot more. And so I allowed these stories to grow up round me. I liked the image. You probably despise me for that, but there it is."

"No, I am not despising," Ghote said.

He found that he was speaking no more than the truth. A few minutes before he might indeed have despised this man if he had known what an act he had been putting on. But the fact that it had been the man himself who had told him of it made him feel very differently.

Yet all the same nothing had been said so far that really cleared him of the Falkland Road crime.

"Go on," he said. "Go on with what you are saying."

"Yes. Yes, I must. Well, if I'm not Krishna romping with those milk-maids or a reincarnation of my beastly grandfather, what am I? Why is it that I've been to that place in Falkland Road, and to some others too before I found it, that I've been to Heera's establishment, how often? Once a month. Sometimes more often, even two or three days in a row. Why is it?"

"I am not at all able to be giving any answer to that."

"No. No, I imagine that you aren't. I hardly can myself. But—but this is the truth of it, Inspector. A truth I thought I'd never have to tell to anyone."

Ghote held his breath.

"Far from being the sort of sadist you must have thought me," the Sheriff said, forcing the words out, "what actually used to go on between Kamla and me was only the most innocent of games. I would play at whipping her, play at it nothing more. And—and she would then play at whipping me. She did not even always touch that whip she had hanging there. Sometimes she did it with her hair. Her hair."

He gave a muffled sob. In part, Ghote guessed, at the pathetic light in which he had revealed himself, in part, surely too, in memory of dead Kamla.

"Yes," he went on, "the same actions, you see, the same physical circumstances but with an absolutely different meaning. A meaning I'm ashamed of having had to tell you. But there it is. It's the truth. The simple, silly truth."

He shuffled a foot on the worn wooden floor.

"I've been caught in your trap, Inspector, and forced to tell it," he said. "You caught me."

Ghote saw that he had done just what the Sheriff had said. He had worked away painstakingly and had caught him in his trap. But what had he caught? Not the wild beast he thought he had set out to capture. Instead the merest tame animal, a man with nothing more sinister about him than a peculiar and rather ridiculous taste in his sexual life. Doubtless a man among a good many similar.

But, if this man was not a wild beast, a beast certainly existed. Kamla's dead body, seen with his own eyes, was witness to that.

So who was this beast?

He certainly believed now that it was not the Sheriff, even though nothing had been said that conclusively disproved the case he had built up. It had been accounted for in part. For instance, as to how the Sheriff's fingerprints had got on to that whip. Had not Munni told him that this visitor had been with Kamla only the day before her death? But otherwise there was still only the Sheriff's assertion that he had arrived at the house and had immediately been warned to leave. The case he himself had built up still existed. Only he himself no longer believed it.

Yet the A.C.P. would. He almost certainly would, and he was on his way at this minute perhaps to effect an arrest. Would he be convinced if he was to tell him what he had heard from the Sheriff's lips just now?

It was unlikely. The A.C.P. was not the sort of person to be much impressed with feelings, especially with his own feelings that the Sheriff had been telling the simple truth about his relations with Kamla.

So what was to be done?

The answer came to him at once. The Sheriff had not killed Kamla but someone else had. And he thought that he knew who that person must be.

If only he could get an admission to it before the A.C.P. had done anything too irrevocable all might yet be well. But there was precious little time. Precious little time.

"Sheriff Sahib," he said. "Stay here. Go and listen again to the music. I am going to see if I can prove what you have told me is true. I am going straight away."

He left the Sheriff standing stock-still in the dim-lit corridor, the white tuberose garland glimmering at his wrist, and hurried off.

17

Outside the Pavan Pool compound Ghote hesitated for a moment.
Should he run back to where his driver was patiently waiting, or
should he make his way on foot? After all, it was hardly very far to go.
To Falkland Road.

He decided not to take the car. At least in that way he would feel
more in control. To be sitting in the car stuck behind some ancient
victoria with a horse incapable of going even as fast as anyone could
run would be intolerable.

At a walk that broke at times into a trot he set out.

His head was awhirl. Everything he had thought of during the case
seemed to have come adrift from its moorings and to be tumbling
round and round looking for a place to slot into.

What had plunged him into turmoil was simple. It was the notion of
the Sheriff not being what he had seemed. At one moment he had
been the beast, the sadist, the maniac killer. And then, without any
real change in outward circumstances, his whole life had appeared as
something entirely different. The very opposite, indeed, of all it had
been the moment before and had seemed to be all during that long
pursuit.

In the light of this transformation thing after thing he had heard
and seen since that first awful moment when he had spotted the
Sheriff of Bombay, no less, leaving a wretched brothel in Falkland
Road had presented themselves with his double face.

He had been aware of that doubleness, too, each time. But he had
entirely failed to grasp the significance of it. To appreciate how something could be utterly different just from the light it was seen in. He
had even been aware of it without realising it just a few minutes ago
when he had listened to the singer in the black sari a second time and
had found the magic gone even though she was singing with every bit
as much beauty and feeling as before.

A man emerging from a shabby Grade III restaurant to comb his hair stepped straight into his path. He shouldered him aside and strode on.

He must get that confession, if he possibly could, before the A.C.P. arrived at the gate of Pavan Pool and began to ask where his inspector was.

He must carry through to the end what he had seen in the light of the Sheriff's topsy-turvying revelation.

It had been there all along, the notion that things were not what they seemed. From the very beginning. From the time the A.C.P. had asked him to escort the Svashbuckler to the Cages. The Cages. They were themselves an echo of the theme. Were they not at once Bombay's pride and its shame? Look at them one way and they were something to take tourists to in an altogether boastful manner. Look at them from the other direction and they were a blot on any city's fair name, a seething mass of squalor.

And the Svashbuckler himself. He had been the subject of just such another switch-over. Meeting him at the Oberoi-Sheraton he had been ready to see a hero. And what had he found? Someone he had not even been able to recognise. A bloated wreck of a man, a feeble fellow who had vomited disgustingly at the merest glimpse of Kamla's dead body.

But more. There had been another switch-over, a switch back, with the Svashbuckler. A switch he himself had actually made happen. He had gone to this non-hero to ask him to confront the Sheriff, but when he had refused it had not been difficult to make him transform himself in his own eyes into a hero again by means of nothing more than a few references to that fake hero he had once been, the man who had faced fake tigers in a fake Indian jungle.

It was all a matter of looking at things from one viewpoint or another. Like that dreadful book of Ved's Protima had found. One moment a disgusting sex manual, the next a *Boys and Girls Book of Facts*. One moment even apparently crammed with pieces of useful information, the next a mishmash of inaccuracies.

A transformation. As it had been with that lightning flash of illumination just now when, with the idea of the Sheriff as Kamla's murderer and as Sweetie Bhaskar's as well suddenly removed, he had seen who alone could be that maniac.

If only he succeeded, in the few minutes he had to do it in, in extracting some sort of confession. In banging it out.

"Sahib, sahib."

Someone he had failed to notice in his hurry, in the confusion of his thoughts, was pulling urgently at his sleeve.

He came to a halt, turned.

It was a beggar, a blind beggar, a scrawny, emaciated fellow dressed in dirt-grimed rags, clutching him hard with one hand while holding out the other, horny and black-traced, for alms.

"*Maaf karo.*"

He jabbed out the old formula begging forgiveness for not being able to bestow charity, tugged his sleeve from the man's grasp and broke into a run.

A few yards only and then he was at the corner of Falkland Road. The street ahead of him was in the full swing of its nightly trade, pavement and roadway thick with strolling, ogling would-be customers.

The pride and the shame of Bombay.

But, whichever it was, there was no hope of getting along it at a run. He would be lucky if he could advance at any more than a shuffle.

From the narrow, blue-barred cage fronts there came the shouts, whistles and hissings of the soliciting whores. From the windows above whores of a higher grade were scarcely less blatant in their attempts to hook the fish swimming in such shoals below.

What was the way in which Dr. Framrose had spoken of them on that fatal first night as he had led the party to Heera's house? That ridiculous comparison with the courtesans of old. Recounting at length, in his high-pitched, attention-catching voice, the recommendations of some ancient writer on what the mother of a courtesan should do to build up her daughter in the very best light. What a contrast there with Heera and the girls to whom she was, in a real way, a sort of mother. A contrast the doctor had been delighted to point up.

Yet, again, that depended on the way you looked. You could look at that courtesan in the book written hundreds of years ago as a figure of crystal. Or you could look on her as being just such another creature to be paid for as . . . As poor dead Kamla.

Nor were the courtesans of today, back there in Pavan Pool, any different. See the best of them from one point of view, as he had done not an hour before, and they seemed unprovoking as statues, moving statues but statues still. Yet see them from only a slightly changed angle and they were little different from—he glanced sideways—from that Nepali girl lounging with the others on the bench just inside the doorway there, dressed in bright red trousers and a body-clinging red top, as blatant a sexual invitation as could be. And indeed any courtesan at Pavan Pool, if only half what that boaster S.I. D'Silva said about them was true, was well capable of coming to an "arrangement" with any man with money enough to have her for a "keep" or of going off for a night when the curfew whistle blew with anyone willing to pay for the privilege.

A victoria, its two absurdly dim coach lamps glowing feebly, presented itself directly in front of him as he made his way with what speed he could down the centre of the roadway. He stepped aside and let it go by, the smell of its horse and ancient, sour straw suddenly strong in his nostrils.

As it at last drew past, his eye was caught by one of the window girls on the opposite side of the street. The light from behind her was falling just across her face. She was looking down at the gawping, chaffering swirl of humanity below with an air of harsh dignity that was, once you had glimpsed it, extraordinarily compelling.

Evidently a whore who hated her trade. Like poor sick Lakshmi from the hut in the Kamatipura lane, or like the girl in Heera's house not so far up the street now, Putla. Putla, the prostitute who often did not open her legs for her clients, who hated the life, who hated them, who hated fat Heera. And who also felt for her as a mother.

See her one way, see her another.

He pushed onwards.

And what a contrast Putla and Lakshmi were to little plump Munni, unable to understand how it could be unpleasant to make "fun" with a whole beguiling variety of men. Or with dead Kamla, the Kolati who had chosen with open eyes the life of a prostitute and who had enjoyed it too. Until she had met with the man he hoped to find within the next few minutes. Yet Putla and Lakshmi, Munni and Kamla could be seen in one light only as prostitutes, however opposed in temperament they were.

Already he could make out the bright glare of the Olympia Café with its ever-moving clientele of street girls and pimps, of pickpockets and policemen, the latter drinking free tea and eating free snacks no doubt, their petty *hafta*.

Unlike Sub-Inspector D'Silva and the fifty-rupee contributions he exacted here, there and everywhere in the red-light area.

A cripple, one-legged and poling himself about with the aid of a long staff, blocked his way. He swung past, angry at even this slight extra delay.

What was a man like that doing here?

And at once the answer came to him. He was doing just what all the other gawpers and idlers were doing. Taking his pick. See him not as a cripple but as a man, and he was a man, a man with the same needs and desires as other men.

But needs which could come and go quickly as the varying images on a cinema screen. As his own need had comprehensively disappeared when he had had to lie naked with Munni as she had told him eventually that the Sheriff had visited Heera's house on the evening before the murder as well as on the day itself, something which he had thought at the time was another link in his chain of proof but which had turned out to be just the opposite, the very fact that innocently accounted for the Sheriff's fingerprints being on the whip he himself had taken away.

Yes, he had had to produce the exact sounds of love-making when the moustached *gharwali* had come into that room. But he had felt nothing. See it one way, see it another.

It was just what the Sheriff had told him about his meetings with Kamla. The same physical circumstances: quite different meanings.

He craned over the shoulder of a tall Pathan walking in front of him and exuding a terrible odour of stale onion to see how near to Heera's house he now was. And there, almost outside it, was Sub-Inspector D'Silva.

He put his head down and forced his way through the mass of onlookers.

Oh yes. D'Silva and his unpleasant tricks. Another instance of transformation. The way he had tried to fool him over the eunuch madam Saroja. And nearly had, too. A man who looked like a woman. See him-her one way, see her-him another.

And that sudden flare-up in the hall of the Sukhlaji Street place, those girls, those whores, asking where respect lay. Respect and a prostitute. Yet, whatever their way of life, they saw themselves as needing respect, as in some way or another perhaps achieving it. The topsy-turvy world. Or again the sealed-bottle girl who was, look at her from a second angle, nothing of the kind, poor little creature. Or another sort of girl changing from one thing to its opposite, the dancers at the Mujra Nite in Colaba, one moment Muslims the next Hindus. Crude transformations hardly deceiving anybody. But making the point all the more forcefully for that. The point he had not then had the sense to see.

D'Silva was coming towards him. Had he noticed him? There was no telling.

He shoved and battered onwards.

Usha Wabgaonkar had been just such another example, too. Wanting respect, wanting a dignified life of a sort, wanting not to be a girl in some office looked down upon, rebuked and snubbed. And choosing to earn respect by losing it, or so to most people it would seem. By losing it as much as it possibly could be lost.

But other eyes, other views. And Usha and Sweetie Bhaskar had, for their different reasons, embraced the call-girl life while seeming to be no more than innocent students, girlish and giggling. While actually still being such gigglers.

How nearly he had made a complete fool of himself in seeing Usha as a giggler only. But it had been from her, though he had not at all realised it until a few minutes ago, that he had had really the one and only valuable clue to naming the man who had murdered her friend Sweetie.

"Hey, it's Ghote again. What are you doing here, *bhai?* Sampling more of the wares?"

D'Silva had spotted him. He was coming right towards him, grinning broadly, all the unpleasantness of their last encounter apparently forgotten.

Or deliberately forgotten. Deliberately seen in some other, easier light?

Ghote took one look at him.

"S.I.," he said, "I am on very urgent business. I will see you later perhaps."

He brushed past him.

Strange to think that, in that first moment of disorienting illumination when he had realised the Sheriff was not at all the monster he had seen him as, he had for an instant wondered whether that monster might be D'Silva. It had really been only because the fellow was always about in Kamatipura and that during that car ride between the Nariman Point brothel flat and Sukhlaji Street he had spoken so highly of "great murderers." Otherwise there had been nothing and, his mind moving rapidly on, he had in the next instant seen who actually the murderer of Kamla and of Sweetie Bhaskar must be.

He took a swift look at Heera's house. The cage girls on its ground floor, much despised by Heera, were looking out, eyeing prospective customers. One of them was shouting to a boy from a tea stall to bring her something to eat. Above, Heera's whores were leaning out of their windows. He saw Putla, the cold-man despiser, looking down disdainfully but nevertheless arranging her sari to show off her splendid body to best advantage. He even caught a glimpse of fat Heera.

Did she know who had killed Kamla? Probably not. She had not been about at the time, and the murderer was a person who could go in and out of the house without inquiry. No, Heera had lied and lied to him only so as to defend her business, to keep off inconvenient inquiries and perhaps too to protect from publicity her most illustrious client, the Sheriff of Bombay.

So, now for the moment of tackling the real monster, of trying to force out of him enough of a confession to make it possible to go back to the A.C.P. and convince him he no longer had to arrest the Sheriff.

Now for Dr. Falli Framrose.

18

Yet was he after all right? The thought presented itself, a looming purple-heavy cloud, in Ghote's mind as he approached Dr. Framrose's dispensary. *Sex Diseases. Sex Changes.*

Its door, he saw, was ajar. The doctor almost certainly would be there. But when he was faced with the brute fact what would be his reaction? Guilty he might be—surely he was guilty—but even so he might well fight back, deny everything, seek to explain each point that told against him. And that would mean delay. At the least.

There would be no hope then of getting back to Pavan Pool before the A.C.P. had waited there for him at the gate too long. Perhaps he would have instituted a search for the Sheriff, found him and without further ado arrested him. What black trouble there would be then. Bad enough simply arresting the Sheriff of Bombay. A thousand times worse arresting him for a crime he had not committed.

Perhaps, even, the Sheriff would soon tire of the entertainment going on in that dingy, blue-walled room, marvellous though it was. Perhaps he would for some reason, as he himself had done earlier, suddenly see it all in a different light. See it as no more than a woman dancing, another singing a meaningless song about roses and lovers and the moon. And then he would set off to leave Pavan Pool. And at the gate he would encounter the A.C.P., and *Sheriff Sahib, it is my grave duty* . . .

Ghote stepped up into the outer room of the bare dispensary. It was empty. The scabby pale green walls looked down on the bare floor. The doctor's umbrella hung from its nail, a tattered black downward-pointing arrow.

"Doctor. Doctor Sahib," Ghote called.

At once Dr. Falli Framrose, Sexologist, F.R.S.H. (U.K.), lath-thin, bald-headed, narrow face blotched with dark patches, large spectacles slipping down his droopy nose, appeared at the doorway from the inner room.

"Ah," he said, "we meet once more. Inspector Ghote, is it not? A consultation, I wonder? Some undesirable symptoms apparent in a delicate region? The inevitable consequence of promiscuous sexual activity, Inspector. I issued a warning. I distinctly recall that I issued you a solemn warning."

Ghote was taken aback. Somehow he had expected the doctor simply to ask him what he wanted, and he had been ready in answer to put a plain accusation and observe the doctor's reaction down to the last detail.

But he did not allow himself to be fazed for long. He could not afford to be.

"No, Doctor," he said, "I am not here for medical advice. Rather it is because of medical advice that you were prepared to offer to someone else."

The doctor did not seem to react to the sombre tone. Yet he had not answered absolutely immediately.

"Really, Inspector, I do not know what you mean. And, if I may say so, I am an extremely busy man. So, if you cannot make yourself more clear, I must ask you to leave me to my work. Heaven knows, the furious activity that is going on all around us at this very hour will bring me in tasks enough."

"Miss Veena Bhaskar," Ghote said bluntly in reply. "Miss Veena Bhaskar, known by the name of Sweetie."

Again there was a pause, tiny but longer than before. It made Ghote one small degree more sure that he was not making a colossal mistake.

"Miss Veena Bhaskar? What of her, Inspector? As far as I am aware I do not know any young person of that name."

"Young person," Ghote snapped in. "How did you know, Doctor, that Miss Bhaskar was a young person?"

"You told me. You must have told me. Or I heard it somewhere. Well, really, Inspector, what are you making such an appalling fuss about? Whether I knew that—that this person was young or old, how can it matter?"

"It is mattering, Doctor, because it proves that you did after all know Miss Sweetie Bhaskar. Miss Bhaskar who was murdered in a circumstance clearly indicating that it was on account of sexual reasons. Miss Bhaskar who was murdered with exactly the same modus operandi as the prostitute Kamla, killed a few doors away only from this dispensary."

Dr. Framrose's spectacles had slipped in his agitation almost to the bottom of his long nose. He pushed them back up again with a single jab of his finger.

"Well, now I know what you have been talking about, Inspector. At least I know that. I was present, if you remember, when that girl's body was discovered. But what connection she can have with this Miss Bhaskar I fail to understand."

"I believe, Doctor," Ghote answered, "that Miss Bhaskar came to consult you because, as a practising call-girl, she had caught a disease. Her very close friend told me it was a lady doctor she had found who would treat her and not tell her parents. But the girl who told me that told also that she herself did not at all know anything about this doctor. At the time I accepted her statement that it was a lady doctor Miss Sweetie Bhaskar had visited because I was made to see it in that light. But now I have come to see that it did not have to be a lady doctor at all. I believe it was a man doctor she had learnt of, and that she had learnt of him because she was working once in this area as an assistant to an American professor of sociology. I believe that doctor was you."

Once more a tell-tale pause before any answer came.

"What if it was me, Inspector? Many young women come to consult me. Prostitutes, call-girls. All the riff-raffs who catch and transmit sexual diseases. I treat them. They go away. And then as often as not they come back. What is this—this Miss Bhaskar to me? And in any case I am not saying that I do know her."

The illogical tirade convinced Ghote yet more strongly that he was on the right track. But how to get some sort of an admission before the A.C.P. found the Sheriff and made that unthinkable arrest?

"What if Miss Sweetie Bhaskar did come to you, Doctor?" he said. "I will tell you what. You are a man who has become obsessed by the sexual act. It is because of the work you do here, no doubt. As you have just told, every day you are treating girls with sexually transmitted disease, and many, many times they are coming back for more treatment when you have cured. So, Doctor, I believe that this has made something to crack in you. The strain and pressures have been altogether too much. And you have decided, with some part of you that you cannot any longer control, that these wicked girls must be punished. You had punished Kamla on the night we first were meeting. You had just come back from killing her, I believe. And after some time when this so-called good girl Sweetie came to you and you found out she was not at all a good girl, you told her that you would treat her in secret and confidence and then you killed her also."

"My dear fellow, what a rigmarole. What nonsense and absurdity. I have never heard anything so ridiculous in all my life."

"No, Doctor, it is not ridiculous. And I can prove that it is not, I do believe. I can prove it by something that was just occurring to me when I was telling about you giving treatment to Miss Sweetie Bhaskar. I saw in my mind then for a moment only just how you would treat her. I saw you in that room inside there opening your drugs cupboard which you were always making such a point of locking up."

"Of course I make a point of locking that cupboard. Of course I do. Of course I do. A drugs cupboard left unlocked in an area of this sort. You must be out of your mind, Inspector. Yes, yes, yes. It is you who are out of your mind. Not me. You, Inspector, out of your mind. Out of your mind."

The words were pouring out. Flecks of saliva had appeared at the corners of the man's mouth.

They were the final sign to Ghote.

"Doctor," he said, "kindly open that drugs cupboard to my inspection."

"No. No, I will not. Why should I? Why should I open it? To a madman. Yes, you are a madman, Inspector. I will report you to your superiors. You will have to be locked up. In a *pagalkhana*. With other lunatics. Yes, locked up. Locked up."

"Doctor, will you open it? Or will I break it open only?"

The doctor suddenly darted back to the inner doorway and planted himself spread-eagled across it.

"What—what do you think you will find in there, Inspector?" he shouted. "What do you think you will find? There is nothing. Nothing. Some drugs only. Drugs needed for treating the demented females who come and come begging for treatment for diseases they are only too ready to go and catch again. What do you think you will find? What? What? What?"

"I will tell you what I expect to find," Ghote answered quietly. "I expect to find the whip that you use, Doctor. The whip that you used to strangle Sweetie Bhaskar and to strangle Kamla, when I thought it was the whip only that was hanging up in Kamla's room. I took that whip away because I was believing that on its very smooth surface fingerprints would be left. Well, yes, there were fingerprints there. But the wounds on that poor girl's back—I can see them now, Doctor. Can you see them also?—they were not the marks of a smooth whip. They were the ridges of a whip made out of thick strips of leather. And it is a whip like that I am expecting to find in your cupboard."

"No."

The doctor had been reduced suddenly from the spate of wild words that had poured out of him before to this one explosive syllable.

It showed that he was calmer, certainly. But, Ghote thought, it might well show too that he was more able to withstand an attack. That he himself was not going to be allowed to get to the drugs cupboard in the next room. From all that had come spewing out of the doctor he was certain now that there was hidden the whip he had used to strangle his two victims, and perhaps others before them.

And that piece of solid evidence he needed.

He stood looking at the thin form of the doctor in front of him, arms spread wide to block the doorway.

What could he do?

Make a fight of it? He would win easily enough against such a frail opponent. But obtaining evidence by violent means was hardly going to look well in court if it came to it. And the struggle and the subsequent forcing of the cupboard's lock might well occupy altogether too many of the few precious minutes left to him.

No, he would not fight. He would try one other last throw.

"Doctor," he said to his now quietly panting adversary, "please to think about yourself. You have been putting up a display that is worthy only of a madcap. You must know this about yourself. The man that you once were, the man that you still are, the doctor, the man who is able to think, must know this. This is the truth, Doctor: you have become two persons. If I see you from one place, you are the doctor, the good man, the helper of those in distress, the scientist also. If I see you from another place, you are a man dedicated to the slaughter of prostitutes, a man who can think of nothing but the evil of sex. Doctor, isn't that what is the case?"

Dr. Framrose made no answer.

It was difficult to see what he was thinking behind his huge spectacles, even though these were in their accustomed way slipping down his droopy nose. But, Ghote thought, it was possible that he had taken in what he had just said, that he was turning it over in his mind.

If only he could produce one argument more to convince him. To tip the balance.

And at once he thought of it.

He dived his hand into his pocket and brought out the little, almost totally forgotten toy he had bought for an extravagant fifty paisa from that tiny bemused boy as he had been going back to Pavan Pool after sending the message that would bring about the Sheriff's arrest. That bargain which, almost as soon as he had slipped it into his pocket, had somehow caused him surely to think that, no, the Sheriff was not the guilty man after all. The little flick-flack picture of a clothed and a naked woman.

"Doctor Sahib," he said, shaking the toy. "Look at this. It will show you just what I am meaning. Look. Look."

He flicked the little rectangle of translucent plastic to and fro in his hand, sure that to the doctor standing blocking his way to that vital piece of evidence it would be showing, first, a woman clothed, next, in the flick of an instant, a woman naked.

The doctor was looking down at his hand.

He flicked the small rectangle again.

"Yes," said the doctor, "I suppose you are right, Inspector. I have become like that absurd thing you are holding. In two minds. In two minds. Oh, very well, go and fetch the wretched whip. My scourge. Yes, my scourge."

Ghote had more than a little difficulty explaining matters to the A.C.P.

To begin with, he had been late in getting back to Pavan Pool. Mercifully the A.C.P. had remained patient, more or less, and had waited at the gate instead of setting out to look for the Sheriff.

But, as it was, Ghote had been only just in time. It had taken him longer than he had counted on to clear up the mess of Dr. Framrose, to find a patrolling constable to take him to Headquarters where he could be properly charged in front of witnesses, to secure other *panches* locally to witness the unlocking of the drugs cupboard, the finding of the whip and its despatch as potential evidence.

So the road outside Pavan Pool had been already jammed with taxis waiting to take away its visitors as he had come running up, sweat-covered in every limb. And just as he had got to the gate the *chowkidar* in his neat forage cap had blown the first blast on his whistle to announce the curfew.

The facts of the case against Dr. Framrose had not been too hard to put, once the A.C.P., his moustache twitching furiously, had vented his annoyance at being kept waiting.

"So," he barked at the end of Ghote's breathless but lucid recital, "so it was that damned doctor, was it? I'd heard some pretty nasty rumours about the fellow. Mad, of course. Apt to say any damn thing that came into his head. One hundred percent a *pagalwalla.*"

"Yes, sir," Ghote said, refraining from further comment as much to get his breathing back to normal as out of circumspection.

"And you wanted me to pull in the Sheriff, Ghote," the A.C.P. went on. "The damn Sheriff of Bombay, and you wanted me to arrest the chap myself on a charge of murder. Of sex murder."

"Sir, I thought the case against him was one hundred—was two hundred percent certain, sir."

"Well, it wasn't, was it? Wasn't even twenty percent, as it turns out."

"No, sir. But it was a question of what point of view you were seeing his activities from, sir."

"Point of view, point of view. You're talking nonsense, Inspector. Either the damn chap was whipping those girls to death or he wasn't. Simple as that. You just had to find out which. Shouldn't have been beyond the powers of a Crime Branch officer."

"No, sir," Ghote said.

He did not think that he could have said anything else.

Inspector D'Sa had managed to rope him in for the *bandobust* of the Vegetable and Flower Show. And, after all, why not? He did not have a great deal of work-load at this time.

So he was there, in uniform, doing nothing much since D'Sa had seen to everything with more than the necessary care, when the Sheriff of Bombay arrived, late, to perform the opening ceremony.

Thinking about the Sheriff beforehand, he had decided that he would do his best not to come face to face with him. When one had had a conversation as appallingly intimate with someone as the talk they had had in the corridor at Pavan Pool it would be more than a little awkward to meet again.

But, thanks to the Sheriff's lateness and D'Sa's fussing about whether they should open the show before it was officially opened or not, he was standing right at the entrance to the roped-off *shamiana,* under whose flag-decorated canvas the many vegetables and few flowers were laid out for inspection, when the Sheriff eventually arrived.

There was no possibility of avoiding him.

So he put a brave face on it.

"Good afternoon, Sheriff Sahib. I am glad to meet you again."

The Sheriff looked at him, an impressively tall figure with his wide, dazzlingly white shirt, the striped tie blazoned across it, carrying easily his lightweight, well-cut suit. His eyes twinkled, carelessly.

"Delighted to see you, my dear—er—"

Ghote saw him glance at the pips on the shoulders of his uniform jacket.

"My dear Inspector. Delighted to see you."

The flash of very white teeth in a meaningless smile and the Sheriff of Bombay had passed by, heading for the cloth-spread table at the top end of the *shamiana,* the cups and the prizes arrayed on it and the heavy garland discreetly hung on the back of a chair ready to be placed round his neck.

Well, Ghote thought, perhaps I should not have expected him to recognise me. Not when I am appearing to be a police officer in uniform. It is all just a matter of what point of view you are seeing somebody from.

Yes, that.

ABOUT THE AUTHOR

H. R. F. KEATING was born in Sussex and educated at Trinity College, Dublin. He began his writing career as a journalist, but after winning the Gold Dagger of the Crime Writers Association in Britain in 1964 and the Edgar Allen Poe Special Award from the Mystery Writers of America, he gave up regular newspaper work. He is now crime book critic for the *Times* in London and writes at least one new mystery a year. Among his previous mysteries are: *A Rush on the Ultimate; Go West, Inspector Ghote; The Murder of the Maharajah;* and *Inspector Ghote Draws a Line.*